Divine Decisions

Divine Cozy Mystery Series
Book 4

Hope Callaghan

hopecallaghan.com

Visit my website for new releases and special offers: hopecallaghan.com/newsletter

D1738800

Contents

Acknowledgments

Thank you to these wonderful ladies who help make my books shine - Peggy H., Cindi G., Jean P., Wanda D., Barbara W., Renate P. and Alix C. for taking the time to preview *Divine Decisions,* for the extra sets of eyes and for catching all of my mistakes.

A special THANKS to my reader review team:

Alice, Alta, Amary, Becky, Brenda, Carolyn, Cassie, Charlene, Christine, Debbie, Denota, Devan, Diann, Grace, Helen, Jo-Ann, Jean M, Judith, Meg, Megan, Linda, Patsy, Polina, Rita, Theresa, Valerie, Virginia and Vicki.

*****

In Memory of Amelia "GiGi" Willard

Cast of Characters

Joanna "Jo" Pepperdine. After suffering a series of heartbreaking events, Jo Pepperdine decides to open a halfway house, for recently released female convicts, just outside the small town of Divine, Kansas. She assembles a small team of new friends and employees to make her dream a reality. Along the way, Jo comes to realize not only has she given some women a new chance at life, but she's also given herself a new lease on life.

Delta Childress. Delta is Jo's second in command. She and Jo become fast friends after Jo hires her to run the bakery and household. Delta is a no-nonsense asset, with a soft spot for the women who arrive broken, homeless, hopeless and needing a hand up. Although Delta isn't keen on becoming involved in the never-ending string of mysteries around town, she finds herself in over her head more often than not.

Raylene Baxter. Raylene is among the first women to come to the farm, after being released from *Central State Women's Penitentiary*. Raylene, a former bond agent/bounty hunter, has a knack for sleuthing out clues and helping Jo catch the bad guys.

Nash Greyson. Nash, Jo's right-hand man, is the calming force in her world of crisis. He's opposed to Jo and Delta sticking their nose into matters better left to the law, but often finds himself right in the thick of things, rescuing Delta and Jo when circumstances careen out of control.

Gary Stein. Gary, a retired farmer, works his magic in Jo's gardens. A widower who finds purpose helping Jo and working on the farm. Gary catches Delta's eye and Jo wonders if there isn't a second chance...at love for Gary and Delta, too.

No weapon formed against you shall prosper; and every tongue which rises against you in judgment you shall condemn. This is the heritage of the servants of the Lord, and their righteousness is from Me, says the Lord." Isaiah 54:17 (NKJV)

Chapter 1

"I can barely move." Delta Childress sucked in her gut and squeezed past a stack of antique books. She was close enough to smell the lingering aroma of vanilla while a rack of vintage evening gowns brushed her backside. "Where is Claire?"

"Buried beneath the rubble," Jo joked. "Claire may have taken on a little more than she can handle for the festival."

The Divine Fall Festival was the talk of the town. Although the festival was new to Jo, according to

Delta, it was the largest event of the year, with visitors flocking from throughout the State of Kansas to their small town for the arts and crafts booths, a livestock auction, carnival rides, a grand parade, and a scavenger hunt, among other things.

Many of the local farmers participated in the Divine Harvest Moon competition, a nighttime harvest. For Delta, the main attraction was the Divine Baking Contest where the grand prize winner would lay claim to not only a trophy but a thousand dollars cash.

Delta had been tweaking her entry for weeks. Their friend, Marlee, the owner of Divine Delicatessen and a previous grand prize winner, was also competing.

Claire popped out from behind an antique curio cabinet, a plumed purple hat perched atop her head. "I do have my hands full, but I love this time of the year. In fact, if you have anything you'd like to sell, I still have a couple of mini-booths available. They're a bargain at twenty bucks for two days."

"Where?" Jo glanced over Claire's shoulder. "I might be interested."

Claire led them to a row of empty shelves not far from the front entrance.

Jo squinted her eyes and studied the three-foot by five-foot shelf. "It's too small." She elbowed Delta. "What do you think? Any ideas on cleaning out a cubby and getting rid of a few things?"

"Get rid of things?" Delta chuckled. "Ever since you and Nash finished the attic book nook you've been pack-ratting. As a matter of fact, I'm almost certain you bought half your treasures right here."

"True. I can't think of anything I want to part with right now. If someone else comes along and wants the open spots, don't wait on me." Jo changed the subject. "Where's the sword you called me about?"

"Back here."

The women followed Claire, weaving their way past display racks crammed full of merchandise to the back counter and cash register. She removed a black case from beneath the cabinet, set it on top and unlatched the cover.

Delta let out a low whistle as she stared at the gold sword, the gem-encrusted handle glinting in the store's fluorescent lights. "Where did you say you got this?"

"At an estate sale. I wasn't even gonna stop but something told me I needed to check it out. The owner is selling everything and moving to a retirement home. I found this on the tippy top of a front porch shelf."

Jo gently lifted the sword, the weight of the weapon taking her by surprise. "It's heavy. There's something etched on the blade."

"I noticed it, too. It looks like a coat of arms. I tried to do a little research online but wasn't able to find much."

"It's definitely unique." Jo studied the inscription on the blade, her eyes traveling to the hilt and the guard. She ran a light hand over the raised portrait on the sword's guard.

"I have a hunch this thing is worth some serious cash," Claire said.

"That would be nice." Jo placed the sword back inside the case. "I hate to see you get your hopes up. It might be nothing."

"I got a good feeling about this piece. I showed it to a couple of other local antique dealers and one of them tried to buy it on the spot."

"We'll find out soon enough." Jo consulted her watch. "Gordon should be here anytime."

Claire had contacted Jo the same day she purchased the sword, asking if she had any connections, someone with more in-depth knowledge of rare antiques.

As luck would have it, Jo's deceased father, the founder of Carlton Oil & Gas, had been a collector of antiques...mainly oil paintings and had purchased most of his artwork through a family friend, Gordon Rastfield.

Jo hadn't spoken to Gordon in years, not since her father's funeral. She'd offered to contact Rastfield, who agreed to take a look at the photos Claire had sent her. Within minutes of Jo forwarding the pictures, the antique expert had called her back, asking if he could inspect the sword in person and had even offered to drive from Kansas City all the way to Divine.

Not only had Gordon offered to make the drive, but he also offered to make it the next morning, which was how Jo and Delta had ended up at Claire's Collectibles and Antiques...to wait for Gordon's arrival.

"Gordon Rastfield. I already checked him out," Claire said. "He's a top-notch antique expert."

The doorbell chimed, and Jo caught a glimpse of Gordon's tall, thin frame as he ducked through the doorway. She hurried to the door to greet him.

"Joanna Pepperdine," Gordon gave her a quick hug, the smile never leaving his face. "I haven't seen you in years. Not since…" his voice trailed off.

"Not since dad's funeral," Jo said. "It's been a few years. You haven't changed a bit."

"I would say the same, but you have changed. You're the spitting image of your mother."

"Thank you. I'll take that as a compliment."

"It was." Gordon peered anxiously over Jo's shoulder. "I can't wait to see the sword."

"It's back here." Jo led him to where Claire and Delta stood waiting. After a brief introduction, she motioned to the black case. "I've already taken a quick look at it. Of course, I'm not nearly as knowledgeable about antiques as you and my father, but it seems to me that Claire might have stumbled upon something."

Claire reached for the lid. "Although I deal in antiques, the age of this particular item has thrown me off. None of my searchable antique databases nor any of the other dealers in the area have expertise in this type of weaponry."

She slowly opened the case.

Gordon's expression grew solemn as he studied the sword. "May I?"

"Yes. Yes, of course."

The man removed a pair of wire-rimmed glasses from his front pocket and slipped them on before carefully removing the sword. He turned it over in his hands as the women waited, quietly watching.

Finally, Jo couldn't stand it any longer. "Do you think this item is a valuable antique?"

Instead of answering Jo's question, Gordon lifted his gaze, his eyes meeting Claire's eyes. "Where did you say you got this?"

"I found it at an estate sale a couple of days ago. It was at an old farm between here and Wichita."

"I see." Gordon grew quiet again as he carefully examined the intricate detailing. He set it back in the case and reached for his cell phone. "I would like to take a few pictures and send them to a friend in Paris, Yves Mercier of Mercier Galleries. He specializes in antique weaponry, particularly of European origins."

"You think this came from Europe?" Claire's eyes grew wide.

"It's possible. Quite possible."

Claire let out a whoop, and Gordon lifted a cautionary hand. "As I said...it's possible. We will know more once we have Yves' opinion. I have a rather odd request."

"Sure. Shoot. Whatever," Claire's grin widened.

"I would like to lift a copy of the sword's inscription."

"You wanna steal this here sword right before our eyes?" Delta, who had so far remained silent, spoke.

"No. He means he wants to rub the surface to get a clearer outline of the inscriptions," Jo explained.

"Exactly," Gordon nodded. "A photograph can catch some of the details, but a sketch will pick up the nuances between the inscriptions."

"You can have whatever you need." Claire yanked open her printer's paper tray, pulled out a few sheets of paper and handed them to Gordon. "Sketch away."

"I brought my own. It's thinner and able to pick up the finer details." Gordon removed a small pad of paper and pencil from his notebook and carefully placed a single sheet on top of the inscription near the tip of the handle.

He lightly ran the pencil across the paper until the inscription became visible. He jotted a number on the sheet, set it off to the side and repeated the process with a second sheet, shifting to the next inscription.

After Gordon finished the sketches, he carefully tucked them in the notepad and slid it back inside the notebook. "These should be sufficient for Yves to give us an opinion." He cast a final look at the sword and slipped his glasses back inside his pocket.

"Here's my card. As soon as I return to my office, I'll send the information to Yves." He handed Claire a business card before flipping the folder shut and began making his way to the door.

Claire hurried after him. Delta and Jo brought up the rear. "When do you think you'll hear back?"

"I'm not sure. There is a time difference, and it depends on Yves' schedule. It could be tomorrow. It could be a couple of weeks. In the meantime, I suggest you find a safe place for the sword." Gordon turned to Jo, the solemn expression gone, and the smile returning. "It's good to see you, Jo. Good to see you looking happy again." He shifted his gaze to the large picture window and Divine's quaint Main Street. "Small town living agrees with you."

"It does," Jo said. "It's good to see you again, too, and under more pleasant circumstances."

"Yes." Gordon patted her arm and turned his attention to Claire. "I'll be in touch."

"Thank you so much." Claire opened the front door. "I appreciate you driving all the way out here to take a look at the sword."

He stepped onto the sidewalk, and Claire stopped him. "Just out of curiosity...what do you think? What are the odds I have a piece of history on my hands?"

"Odds?" Gordon chuckled. "Odds are only that, but if I have to guess it's fifty-fifty."

"Fifty-fifty," Claire repeated. "I'll take it."

After Gordon left, the women made their way back inside.

Jo watched as Claire locked the case and slid it back under the cabinet. "Are you going to take the sword home with you?"

"Yeah. I'm closing over at the laundromat tonight. After I'm done, I'll stop back by here and grab it." Claire thanked Jo again for arranging to have Gordon inspect the sword and then Delta and Jo returned to the car for the drive home.

"I've been meaning to ask you - have you ever heard the women mention a man named Curtis?" Delta asked.

"Curtis?" Jo wrinkled her nose. "No. Not that I can recall, but then you spend more time with them than I do. Is he a customer?"

"I don't know. I caught Tara and Sherry talking about someone named Curtis and how they're keeping an eye on him. When I asked them about it, they clammed up."

"Interesting. I'll keep my ears open."

They coasted past Marlee's deli and stopped when they reached the corner.

A baby blue Lincoln Continental turned onto the street, careening over the centerline, almost clipping the front corner of Jo's SUV before roaring off, the tires squealing.

"Did you see that?" Delta's head snapped back.

"Yeah. The driver was in my lane. She nearly clipped our front corner."

"No." Delta struggled to look behind her. "It's her."

"Her...who?" Jo shook her head, confused.

"Amelia Willis."

"Who is Amelia Willis?"

"I wonder if Marlee knows," Delta said. "I can't believe it. And now...of all of the times to come cruising back into town."

"I don't know who Amelia Willis is, but she's sure got you in a tizzy."

"She's an old friend...well, a frenemy. And one of the best bakers in all of Smith County. She's here for the contest." Delta rattled on about Amelia, her baking prowess and how she'd moved away several years ago.

"Maybe she's moving back," Jo interrupted.

"Just in time to throw a wrench in my foolproof plan to win the baking contest," Delta grumbled. "I might as well pull out of the competition. Amelia is gonna win."

"No, she's not," Jo said. "And you're not pulling out of the contest. You have just as much chance to win as Amelia or even Marlee for that matter."

When they reached the farm, a glum Delta climbed out of the SUV and tromped across the yard, up the steps and into the kitchen. By the time Jo caught up with her, she was already on the phone with Marlee.

From the one-sided conversation, Jo surmised Marlee was just as surprised by Amelia's unexpected arrival as Delta was. She waited for her friend to end the call.

"Amelia already stopped by the deli to say 'hi.'"

"I bet Marlee isn't pulling out of the contest."

"No, but she's worried. I could hear it in her voice," Delta sighed heavily and reached for her apron.

"Competition is healthy...it's a good thing."

"We'll see."

Despite Jo's attempts to cheer Delta up, she was in a sour mood the rest of the afternoon and evening. Even the women who lived at the home noticed and tiptoed around her.

Nash arrived late for the meal and joined them as they were finishing their desserts. The others began helping Delta clear the table while Jo stayed behind to catch up. "How are the repairs to the tool shed going?"

"Fine. I need a few more supplies. I'll pick them up tomorrow at the hardware store," Nash said. "Delta's in a fine mood. I guess she heard Amelia Willis is back in town."

"Yep. We nearly collided with her earlier. Delta is fit to be tied. I guess they're sort of friends, with a heavy dose of friendly competition."

"Amelia is a real sweetheart. I bet she's heard all about Second Chance. She'll be 'roundabout soon so you can meet her yourself." Nash polished off the rest of his meatloaf and reached for his napkin. "I was thinking about the festival. How do you feel about fairs and festivals?"

"I haven't been to one in years," Jo confessed.

"I was thinking maybe you and I could check it out together Saturday night."

Jo's heart did a mini flip as their eyes met. "I would like that."

Nash cleared his throat. "Good. I mean, you don't have to feel pressured to say yes. You could just tell me no."

"Are you trying to back out of our date already?" Jo teased.

A tinge of pink crept into Nash's cheeks. "No." He shifted uncomfortably. "I'm not sure about the rules on asking my boss for a date."

"I don't believe there are rules," Jo said softly. "We can..."

Delta burst into the room, and Jo jerked back.

"Sorry. I didn't mean to interrupt." Delta began waving Jo's phone. "Your cell phone is blowing up. When I grabbed it, I happened to glance at the screen. I think you might want to take this call."

Chapter 2

Before Jo could grab the cell phone from Delta, it stopped ringing. "I missed it."

"I wasn't trying to snoop, but I did see it was Chris Nyles."

Jo's heart skipped a beat. "Chris. I'm sure he's calling about Miles Parker."

A private investigator had shown up on Jo's doorstep a few weeks ago claiming he was representing a client who was looking for her. After confirming her identity, the detective had been vague, only stating that his client would be in contact.

Not long after, Miles Parker arrived at Jo's farm, claiming to be her half-brother and stating that they shared the same father. Before he left, Parker threw around some vague threats about taking Jo's farm and a chunk of her substantial inheritance.

In a panic, Jo contacted Chris, an attorney and family friend. At Jo's request, Chris had done some investigating into Parker's claim and had reported back with the disturbing news that Mr. Parker could possibly be related to Jo.

Jo's initial reaction was to pay Miles Parker to go away, but after giving it some thought and at the advice of both Chris and Delta, she decided to wait to see if...or when Miles would surface again.

It had been quiet since the initial contact, and Jo was beginning to think Parker didn't have a legitimate claim.

"It looks like he left a message." Jo listened to the brief message from the attorney, asking her to give him a call. "I had better call him back. It sounds important."

Nash abruptly stood. "I can go."

Jo motioned for him and Delta to stay. "No. You both know where I'm at. I would like you to stay if you want."

"Absolutely," Nash resumed his position.

Delta patted Jo's shoulder before plopping down in an empty chair. "We're in this together. Maybe he has good news."

"Maybe." Jo attempted a half-hearted smile before dialing Chris's personal cell phone.

"Hey, Jo. That was quick."

"I just missed your call. I was thinking about you the other day, thinking how lucky I was I hadn't heard back from you," she joked. "No news is good news."

"Yes." Chris cleared his throat. "Unfortunately, I do have some news."

Jo began to feel lightheaded. She knew Chris well enough to detect the note of concern in his voice.

"Miles Parker and I are related. He has some sort of proof that he's my half-brother."

"Not quite. Parker's attorney contacted my office this morning. They would like permission to gather DNA samples to verify if there's a match between your father and Mr. Parker."

Jo's mind drew a blank as she attempted to process Chris's statements. "DNA samples from my father. You mean they want to dig him up?"

"It would be much easier on Parker and his attorney if you agreed to supply a DNA sample instead of attempting to obtain one from your father."

"I see." Jo began to pace. "What if I don't...agree to provide a DNA sample?"

There was a brief pause on the other end of the line. "The decision is entirely up to you, Jo. If you don't agree to a sample, my guess is their next step would be to petition the courts to exhume your father's body."

He continued. "Like I said, the decision is up to you. I told Mr. Parker's attorney I would get back with him in the next day or so."

"They must believe there's a good chance Miles is my half-brother," Jo rubbed her brow. "Otherwise, why go to all of this trouble?"

"Correct." Chris let out a heavy sigh. "We both know there's a lot at stake. I'm sure your father never dreamed this would happen, but it has."

"Yes, it has," Jo echoed. "Before I give you an answer, I would like to give it some thought."

"I wouldn't expect anything less. Just give me a call when you've made a decision."

"I will." Jo thanked him and then started to hang up. "Wait! Chris."

"Yes, Jo?"

"Let's say I go ahead and agree to DNA testing; the results confirm Parker and I are related. What happens next?"

"Then the ball is in their court," Chris said. "If, or when, the time comes, I'm sure they'll let us know Parker's intentions."

"That's what I'm afraid of." Jo thanked him again and promised to get back with him before hanging up.

Delta was the first to speak. "I'm sorry, Jo. This wasn't the news we were hoping for."

"Right." She tossed the phone on the table. "You both caught the gist of the conversation. Miles Parker and his attorney are asking me to provide DNA for testing. If I don't, Chris believes their next step would be to petition the courts to exhume my father's body."

"What are you going to do?" Nash asked quietly.

"I don't see how I have a choice. Either way, it sounds as if Parker will get the DNA sample with or without me." Jo wandered over to the window and stared out at the evening sky, a breathtaking burst of deep purple hues.

A tiny piece of Jo wanted to refuse the request, to make Miles Parker work for what he believed was rightfully his and not hand him the results on a silver platter. The reasonable part of Jo thought if she tried to stay on amicable terms, if the results revealed they were related, he might be inclined to agree to a fair settlement.

She spun on her heel. "I think I'll go ahead and give the sample. I'll let Chris know tomorrow, after I sleep on it."

"You're a kinder woman than me." Delta swiped an imaginary crumb off the dining room table. "I would make him wiggle and squirm for a while. He's been hanging around town, taunting you from day one and even going as far as threatening to take this place."

"It will never happen," Jo vowed. "I will fight with every red cent I have to keep the farm." She turned to Nash. "Delta says fight. I say try to remain on civil terms. What do you think?"

Nash shifted in his chair. "I can see both sides. On the one hand, I don't think he deserves a dime, but the courts may see it differently. You can catch more flies with honey than vinegar."

"That's my thought. I don't want to battle Parker if he has a legitimate claim. Nor do I want him to think I'm going to roll over and hand him everything because I have no intention of doing that. I'll go ahead with the DNA. In the meantime, I'll start doing a little online research to figure out how the courts typically rule in cases like this."

Nash finished his meal, grabbed his dirty dishes and headed to the kitchen. Delta hung back, staring at her friend. "This is your decision, Jo. I'm behind you one hundred percent no matter what you decide."

"Thanks, Delta. I'm going to need all of the support I can get until this mess ends." Jo changed the subject. "What else did Marlee have to say about your friend's arrival?"

"Like I mentioned earlier, Amelia already stopped by the delicatessen to say 'hello' to Marlee. Just as I suspected, she's gonna stay in town until after the fall festival. Ten bucks says she plans to enter the contest."

"I'm sure there's a deadline for entries," Jo pointed out.

"Yes, ma'am. The cutoff is the day after tomorrow. Amelia has until then to throw her recipe into the ring. I can't believe that after all this time and out-of-the-blue she decides to breeze right back into town."

"You have just as much chance of winning the baking contest as Amelia...and Marlee for that matter."

Delta made an unhappy sound as she trudged toward the kitchen. "We'll see." She passed by Nash on his way out, and Jo followed him to the porch.

"Are we still on for our Saturday date?" Jo asked.

"Yes." Nash nodded. "I'm a little rusty at the dating scene. I'm sorry if my invitation came off as sloppy."

"You may be rusty, but I'm darn near a dinosaur as far as dating goes."

"We'll see about that." Nash leaned close, so close Jo caught a whiff of his spicy cologne before he abruptly jerked back. "I better get going." He sauntered down the steps and began whistling as he crossed the drive, and then disappeared inside his workshop.

The front door banged shut, and Delta joined her. "Were you and Nash smooching?"

"Smooching? No." Jo sucked in a breath. "He leaned in like he was going to say something and then he took off. He asked me to the festival."

"A date," Delta clapped her hands. "Whoee."

"Yes, but it's *only* a date." Jo's smile faded. "I think I'm gonna hop in the truck and go for a ride. This whole Parker thing has me rattled. Maybe a long drive with the windows rolled down, and some fresh country air will settle my nerves."

Jo let out a sharp whistle. "C'mon, Duke. Let's go for a ride in the truck."

Duke, Jo's hound dog, darted past her and across the driveway to the pickup while she followed Delta inside. Jo snatched the keys off the hook and then walked out the back door before joining her pup near the cab of the truck.

"Hop in." Duke scrambled onto the seat and took his favorite spot on the other side. After starting the truck, she turned onto the road and headed in the opposite direction of town.

As she drove, her thoughts bounced from her farm, home to six former female convicts who were eager for a second chance, to Nash's unexpected invitation, to Miles Parker's shocking claim and finally...her father's death at the hands of Jo's mother.

It had taken Joanna Pepperdine years to work through her anger and grief. Her halfway house had been a huge step in the healing process.

For the first time in years...decades, she was finally beginning to put her life back together, finally forgiving her father for his infidelities, for the years of physical and emotional abuse her mother had suffered at her father's hands.

Last, but not least, she finally stopped blaming herself for what had happened. Miles Parker's arrival had ripped open the old wounds, and the waves of grief were as new as the day of her father, Andrew Carlton's, death.

Jo drove aimlessly up one country road and down another until the evening light faded and it was dark. Certain Delta would be worried since she'd been gone for a couple of hours, she turned around and headed toward the farm. The front porch lights blazed brightly, beckoning her back home.

She eased into the empty parking spot and shut the engine off. Only then did Jo realize she'd left both her purse and cell phone behind.

Delta greeted Duke and her at the door, a concerned look on her face. "I've been worried sick about you." She watched as Jo hung the spare set of truck keys on the hook.

"I'm sorry. I was so distracted I forgot my purse and cell phone."

"Claire just called."

"Let me guess...she found another treasure she wants Gordon to appraise."

"No. Someone broke into the antique shop and stole the sword."

Chapter 3

Jo's eyes widened. "You mean to tell me someone took the sword right from under Claire's nose?"

"Just about. She was in the laundromat working the last couple of hours before closing and planned to go back to get the sword before heading home," Delta said. "Someone picked the lock on the cellar doors, broke into the antique shop and stole the sword."

Delta explained Claire had already called the police, who showed up to investigate. "The sword was hidden underneath the cabinet, right where she left it when we were there."

"This is terrible," Jo said. "Claire must be beside herself."

"She's heartbroken."

Jo tried her friend's cell phone. Claire didn't answer, so she left a brief message. "I'll run by there in the morning to see if there's anything I can do to help. I think I'll go check on the women. They've been unusually quiet the last few days. Something's up."

"Curtis. That's what's up. I heard his name mentioned again when the women were clearing the dinner table." Delta hung her apron on the hook near the door. "I'll go with you."

Delta and Jo crossed through the backyard to the women's apartments in the back. The resident's housing, a long, low building, was directly behind the mercantile. The individual units consisted of six apartments, three on each side. In the center, and separating the apartments, was the common area.

The women had nicknamed the shared area the "Palace." It sported a fully equipped kitchenette and a large round dining room table. On the other side of the open area, there was a cozy living room with overstuffed lounge chairs and a sectional sofa.

A set of desks and laptops were in one corner. Beyond the living room were two bathrooms, each sporting a spacious shower and an individual toilet stall.

Upon arrival, the residents were assigned a medicine cabinet for their personal hygiene products and were given a lock and key to secure their belongings.

"I see 'em." Delta peeked in the Palace's kitchen window before opening the door and stepping inside.

Kelli took one look at Jo and Delta and darted to the bathroom, returning moments later. The others were seated around the dining room table. The table was filled with makeup and cosmetics.

"What's going on?"

"We're having a makeup session." Tara waved a mascara wand in their direction. "I took some makeup classes back in the day and asked the others if I could practice on them."

"I see." Jo's eyes twinkled with mischief as she pointed at Delta. "I think Delta would like her makeup done."

Delta shot Jo a horrified look. "No, ma'am. I don't touch the stuff. It gives me hives. Literally. I swear if that stuff comes anywhere near my skin I'll break out in an itchy red rash."

Tara looked crestfallen.

"Perhaps you could give me a mini-makeover," Jo offered.

"Awesome." Tara brightened as she led Jo to an empty chair. "You can sit here." She pulled several trays of makeup across the table and arranged them in a semi-circle.

Jo closed her eyes as Tara began applying a thick layer of foundation.

Next, she dusted a light coating of shimmering powder along her cheekbones and then began dabbing at Jo's eyelashes with a mascara wand.

While Tara worked, she chattered on about her plans to move to New York City and snag a job on Broadway doing makeup for the showbiz elites.

Yow.

"I heard something." Jo jerked her head in the direction of the noise. "Did you hear that?"

"Hear, hear...what?" Sherry stuttered.

Yowww.

"That sound." Jo motioned for Tara to stop. "It sounds like an animal in pain."

"I heard it, too." Delta, determined to track down the source of the racket, marched toward the bathroom door. "It's comin' from over here."

YOWWWLL.

Delta flung the bathroom door open.

A black ball of fur dashed out of the room. The furball barreled across the tile floor, colliding with the back of Jo's chair.

"You have a cat."

"It's a kitten," Kelli twined her fingers. "Tara found him in the barn yesterday morning. He was starving, so we brought him home and fed him."

"A kitten." Delta scooped up the small creature. "Poor fella. He's nothin' but skin and bones. Miss Delta's gonna have to fatten you up," she cooed.

"Does that mean we can keep him?" Raylene asked. "We...weren't sure how well you liked pets. I mean, not counting Duke."

"He's just as cute as a button." Delta held him up for a quick inspection and then handed him to Jo.

The kitten began to purr, butting his head on the bottom of Jo's chin. "He is a scrawny little guy. Someone must've dropped him off."

The kitten pawed at Jo's finger nibbling the end, and her heart melted. She gazed around the room, noting the hopeful looks on the women's faces. "I love animals. We certainly don't need a farm full, but I don't see why we can't add one more to the family."

"Sweet." Leah clapped her hands. "You're going to fall in love with him."

"Thanks, Jo," Kelli said. "We were going to tell you about Curtis earlier, but figured you had kind of a rough day, so we thought we would wait until tomorrow."

"Curtis," Jo repeated his name.

"This is Curtis?" Delta roared. "I've heard you mention Curtis's name. I thought you were talkin' about a man."

"A man?" Kelli laughed.

"We have enough troubles without adding men to the mix," Sherry quipped.

Curtis began squirming, and Jo gently set him on the floor. He charged across the room and hopped on Delta's shoe. "Curtis. Let's go rustle up a snack.

We'll have to go easy on the food or else you're gonna get sicker than a dog."

Delta and Curtis departed, and the conversation turned to the upcoming fall festival.

"Speaking of the festival." Kelli snapped her fingers. "I almost forgot. Our merchandise came in today." She ran out of the room, returning a short time later carrying a brown box and set it on the table. "I hope you like them."

Kelli, one of the more creative residents, had been hard at work designing souvenirs and trinkets for Jo's store, Second Chance Mercantile.

She handed Jo a brightly colored sunflower magnet, its face tilting upward toward the sun in the corner. A field of green grass was below the sunflowers, and the words "Divine, Kansas" were etched across the bottom of the grass.

"It's a beautiful magnet," Jo said. "I think we'll sell out of these fast."

Delta and Curtis returned. "This fella is gonna be a big eater and a good mouser. Curtis the mouser." She set him on the rug and made her way over to the table. "What's that?"

"The souvenirs Kelli designed." Jo passed the magnet to Delta.

"We also ordered ink pens and a custom cookie cutter for our bakeshop. The vendor can even create custom aprons with the same print." Kelli handed Jo a sheet of paper. "This is their pricing."

Jo studied the sheet. "The prices seem reasonable. Minimum order is a dozen. Why don't we put the pens and magnets in the store in the morning and then order a dozen aprons to see how they sell since it's a higher-ticket item?"

"Really?" Kelli beamed. "You're not just saying that?"

"I'll take me an apron," Delta said. "You got an eye for design, Kelli. These are very eye-catching."

"I agree," Raylene reached for the pen. "These will sell like hotcakes."

"Your transformation is complete." Tara set the makeup brush on the table and handed Jo a mirror. "I hope you like it."

Jo almost dropped the mirror when she caught a glimpse of the unfamiliar face staring back at her. Although she wasn't opposed to makeup, she never bothered with it since she spent most of her time at the farm.

Even in her younger years, she hadn't been like most of her friends who spent hours primping.

"Joanna Pepperdine." Delta leaned in; her eyes wide. "I hardly recognize you."

"In a good way, I hope."

"You look like you're ready for a night on the town," Raylene said. "The eyeshadow Tara used gives your gray eyes a certain sparkle."

"Thank you, Tara. You have a special talent, and I think it's something you should pursue."

"I...thanks, Jo. Your opinion means a lot," Tara said.

Before leaving, Jo promised Kelli she would place an order for the aprons the next day. She thanked Tara for the makeover, and then Delta and she started back toward the house.

"Well?" Delta waited until the door was shut and they were out of earshot.

"Well, what?"

"Tara. She seems to be settling down."

Tara was the newest member of the household. She'd recently confessed to Jo that she wasn't sure how she fit in since she was more of a "city girl." Like the others, the young woman had a troubled past, including arrests for prostitution and drug possession. Her most recent incarceration came after a conviction for her involvement in an armed robbery she and her former boyfriend had committed.

At first, Jo had been on the fence about allowing Tara to live at the farm when Pastor Murphy had approached her, but after meeting the young woman during a visit to the Central State Women's Penitentiary, she changed her mind.

Her change of heart came after discovering Tara was desperate to turn her life around and gain custody or at a minimum, visitation rights, of her daughter, who was being cared for by her parents in Chicago.

Tara's comment about being a city girl concerned Jo, and she'd made a point of keeping a close eye on the woman. Despite her concerns, so far Tara had fit in nicely with the others and seemed to get along.

"Yes," Jo agreed. "Tara does get along with the other women, and to be honest she has livened up the place a bit." She rubbed the tip of her index finger across the thick layer of makeup. "Tara hasn't mentioned contacting her family in Chicago."

"But she will," Delta predicted.

"Yes. I'm almost afraid to encourage the women to contact their families. You know what happened the last time I tried to help. It blew up in my face."

"You can't blame yourself for Sherry's parents. Sherry knew going into it that her father might not be receptive."

"I know, but I hoped after all of these years her family would at least hear her out," Jo said. "Life's too short to die with bitterness and anger in your heart."

"Amen to that."

The women had reached the back door, and Delta held it open while Jo stepped inside. "I can't help but think about poor Claire's burglary. It sounds like the thief knew exactly what they were after and where to find it."

"Stands to reason," Delta agreed.

"Claire never called me back. I'll get ahold of her in the morning." Before heading upstairs, Jo let Duke out for a quick bathroom break.

She grabbed her pajamas and made a beeline for the master bathroom. Despite the evening's distractions, including Claire's theft, what weighed heaviest on Jo's mind were Miles Parker and the DNA test results.

Should she go ahead and agree to provide a sample to see if there was a match? Chris had told her she could refuse, forcing Parker and his attorney to jump through hoops to petition the courts to exhume her father's body.

Jo loved the Lord with all of her heart and tried her best to love others, to share her faith by showing her faith through her actions. But there was the tiniest black spot on her heart...the thought it would serve her father right to have someone who might be his own son, disturb his final resting place.

She was disappointed in herself for even thinking the thought. Jo reached for a clean washrag and began scrubbing her face. As she scrubbed, she decided the right thing to do was to agree to provide a sample and let the chips fall where they may.

The decision gave her a sense of peace, and she prayed for God's will to be done in the situation. Regardless of the outcome, He could use what was happening to her now as a lesson for not only Jo and the women who looked up to her for guidance, but perhaps even for Miles Parker.

Jo patted Duke's head before rolling onto her side and pulling the covers up around her. Either way, Joanna Pepperdine's life was, once again, about to change.

Chapter 4

By the time Jo was up and ready for the day, Delta's morning assistant, Leah, was putting the finishing touches on a hearty breakfast while Delta finished a batch of blueberry crumble muffins earmarked for Divine Baked Goods Shop.

According to some of the locals, business would be booming during the fall season and slowly tapering off after the weather cooled and fewer people visited the area to see the main attraction...the center of the contiguous lower forty-eight United States.

There wasn't much to the tourist spot except for a large sign and a small church. Jo had visited the spot not long after purchasing her farm. The fact there wasn't much to see didn't deter the tourists who came in droves to take selfies and check it off their bucket lists.

The stories of angelic visitations were more fascinating to Jo than living smack dab in the center of the country was. She thought about her resident, Raylene's, angelic encounter and how the angels had saved her life after she jumped off Divine Bridge, intending to end her life.

Jo believed Raylene had experienced a Divine Intervention, and that God wasn't done with her yet. There were other stories of locals experiencing a divine encounter.

Not long after purchasing the farm, Jo had what she believed was her own personal divine encounter, when a small fire started in her bedroom and she'd been shaken awake...literally.

At the time, she hadn't thought much about it, but after hearing the stories of angelic encounters, Jo was convinced God had saved her life.

She suspected she'd had a second encounter during a recent inspection of the gardens out back when Jo had noticed two unusually large and muscular men standing on the other side of her fence.

Curious to find out what the men were doing, she started to make her way over when bright sunlight had suddenly blinded her. After her vision cleared, she looked again, and the men had simply vanished into thin air.

Delta turned as Jo tiptoed into the kitchen and did a double take. "You're up early this morning."

"I need to check the mercantile inventory. I promised Kelli I would order the aprons for the store and then I want to head into town to talk to Claire."

"I'll go with you if you don't mind." Delta removed a pan of muffins from the oven and set them on top of the stove. "I wanna stop by Marlee's deli to get the scoop on Amelia."

"Are you still worried about the woman? Seriously, she can't be that awesome of a baker."

"I'm at a concerned level. Worried would be if Amelia plans to enter her strawberry cake in the baking contest. It's a little slice of heaven." Delta smacked her lips, a faraway expression on her face. "Pure bliss, the ripe berries, the creamy sauce, pooled in the center of a moist Bundt cake of tasty deliciousness."

"So, she makes a good cake," Jo shrugged. "Amelia has met her match. Your raspberry dream bars are divine."

The rest of the residents, along with Nash began gathering in the dining room while Delta, Leah and Jo carried the dishes of food to the table.

Family meals were the highlight of Jo's day. She looked forward to chatting with the residents not only to get a feel for life at the farm, but also to get their thoughts on the bakeshop and mercantile.

And she loved how each of the women was growing day-by-day, eager to share their talents and move forward with their new lives.

Jo's gaze circled the table. Kelli, the farm's artistic resident, was first. Tara was the city girl. Leah was the exact opposite of Tara, a country girl at heart who planned to own a sustainable farm someday. Michelle was the timid one, who had low self-confidence, something Jo was working on with her. Raylene, a former bounty hunter, had gone through a lot and had even helped Jo solve a recent murder.

Last, but not least, was Sherry, who had been with Jo the longest. Sherry had recently taken a job at Marlee's deli. She was the resident closest to being ready to spread her wings and fly the coop. During a recent conversation, she'd confided in Jo that she wanted to stay in Divine, something Jo encouraged after her recent heartbreaking rejection by her family.

The women and Nash bantered back and forth, chatting about the upcoming day and telling him about Curtis.

After breakfast ended, the women helped clear the table while Jo followed Nash onto the front porch. "Who's working with you today?"

"Michelle. What's on your schedule?"

Jo rattled off her to-do list. "Before I start, I'm going to run into town. Someone broke into Claire's antique shop last night and stole a sword."

"No kidding." Nash raised a brow.

Jo told him how Claire had taken pictures of the sword, and then Jo had sent them to a well-respected antique dealer she knew. "Gordon thinks it may be valuable. The only problem is...now it's missing." She stared at him thoughtfully. "I've been thinking about it. Claire told me she showed it to a couple of other local antique dealers."

"Which means one of them may have realized the potential worth and decided to help themselves."

Michelle joined them. "I'm ready to start my day."

"Good." Nash gave her a warm smile. "I'll be right there." He waited for Michelle to leave before turning his attention back to Jo. "I saw Duke and you head out in the truck last night."

"I decided to go for a drive to clear my head and give some thought to Miles and his attorney's request."

"And?"

"I'm going to go ahead and provide the DNA sample."

"I figured you would," Nash said. "God's got this."

"Yes. He sure has. I better let you get to work." Jo watched him cross the driveway to his workshop and started to make her way back inside when she noticed a Smith County patrol car pull into the drive. It was Deputy Brian Franklin.

She stepped off the porch and waited for him to join her. "Are you here to pick up some of Delta's delicious apple cider donuts?" Jo teased. "She whipped up a batch yesterday, and they're flying off the shelves."

"I might have to pick me up a few." The young deputy shifted uncomfortably. "Unfortunately, this isn't a social call or even a stop to shop for Delta's delectable treats. I'm here to ask you a few questions about Claire Harcourt and a recent burglary at her antique shop."

"I heard," Jo shook her head. "I haven't spoken to Claire, but Delta told me she was working at her laundromat when someone broke into the antique shop and stole a potentially valuable item."

"Yes." The deputy removed a notepad and pen from his pocket. "Claire also mentioned you arranged for a Kansas City antique dealer to give his opinion on the worth of a sword."

"I did." Jo explained how she'd forwarded pictures to Gordon. "He must have thought there was a chance Claire had purchased something of significant value. He drove straight down, examined the sword and then left."

"How well do you know this dealer…"

"Gordon Rastfield," Jo said. "My father was an art collector. Gordon is a highly regarded collector, and his reputation is impeccable. He was also a family friend."

"But he was one of the few people who knew the potential value of the sword," the deputy prompted.

"Yes, he was," Jo said. "You can contact Gordon yourself, but I'm sure he was back in Kansas City by the time the thief broke into Claire's place. He left his business card with her."

"I have his contact information." The deputy stopped writing. "Where were you last evening around eight o'clock?"

Jo's eyes widened. "Me? You think I broke into Claire's place and took the sword? That's absurd."

The deputy ignored her comment. "Can you confirm your whereabouts last evening between eight and ten p.m.?"

"I…" Jo remembered her long drive the previous evening to clear her head. "Actually, I took a long drive after dinner last night. I think I returned around nine or so."

"Alone?" The deputy began scribbling furiously.

"Yes. Alone. Unless you count my dog, Duke. I can assure you I wasn't anywhere near downtown Divine or Claire's antique shop, and even if I was, I would never break into my friend's business and steal from her."

The deputy stopped writing and tapped the top of his notepad. "I'm sorry, Jo. I have to follow up on all leads."

Jo pressed a hand to her chest. "Claire doesn't think I'm responsible, does she?"

"No. In fact, she was reluctant to mention you saw the sword except for the fact Mr. Rastfield made a special trip to Divine to view it."

Relieved her friend didn't suspect her, Jo had barely released the breath she was holding.

"But now that you don't have an alibi for your whereabouts during the time in question, I need to talk to Delta who was with you and Claire, as well."

"Of course." Jo motioned for the deputy to follow her to the house, up the front steps and inside.

"You got this place looking real nice, Jo," the deputy complimented. "It's a shame someone claiming to be related to you is threatening to take it."

Jo stopped in her tracks. "How did you hear about Miles Parker?"

Deputy Franklin shrugged. "Gossip. He was in town a couple weeks ago, shooting off his mouth, telling some of the store owners that soon he would own half the town of Divine, once he took over the farm and claimed his rightful share of the Carlton Oil & Gas wealth."

"He told people in town that?" Jo could feel the blood drain from her face, horrified at the thought

Parker – a complete stranger – had aired her dirty laundry to the townsfolk.

"I'm sorry, Jo. I thought you knew."

"I had no idea. Besides, I don't know if Parker's claim is true." Their eyes met, and it dawned on Jo why the young deputy had shown up on her doorstep. "You think since Miles Parker is claiming he plans to take my money; I may have been looking for a way to make some quick cash to pay him off and decided to steal the sword."

Deputy Parker hung his head, and Jo knew her guess was spot on. "You can tell all of the local townspeople I have more than enough money to take care of Miles Parker. I have no plans to hand over the farm to him and no plans to close Second Chance."

"What's going on?" Delta hurried into the living room. "I thought I heard your voice, Deputy Franklin."

"He's here to ask me about Claire's theft. I'm guessing I'm a suspect now that I don't have an alibi from my whereabouts last night and since I'm in desperate need of quick cash to pay Miles Parker to go away."

"What?" Delta's jaw dropped. "Surely, Claire doesn't believe you're responsible for the missing sword."

"No. Not Claire but someone else." Jo pinned the deputy with a pointed stare. "The whole town knows about Parker's claim. He's going around telling people he plans to take my farm and my inheritance."

"He's full of manure," Delta said. "Someone oughta sew that troublesome man's lips shut. Maybe I can help him out with that."

Despite Jo's aggravation, the mental image of Delta sewing Miles's lips together made her smile. It quickly vanished. "So now I'm a suspect."

"I know you women are busy, but I have a couple of questions for you too, Delta." The deputy asked Delta to recount her hours from the time she and Jo visited Claire at the antique shop to the time Jo returned from her evening drive.

Since several of the women and Nash could confirm Delta's claim that she was at the farm the entire evening, his questioning was brief.

Deputy Franklin flipped the notebook shut and tucked it inside his top pocket. "Sheriff Franklin is questioning some of the other local antique dealers who also knew about the sword."

"I would focus my attention on them," Jo said.

"We are, Jo. I'm sorry to have to involve you in this." The deputy thanked them for their time and exited the house.

Jo watched him climb into his patrol car, back out of the drive and pull onto the main road. "Did you know Miles Parker was going around airing my dirty laundry?"

"No." Delta sighed heavily. "But I'm not surprised. He's a troublemaker. You sure you're still on board with providing a DNA sample?"

"I was going to, but I'm so ticked off right now I'm having second thoughts. At the very least, I'm going to let Parker sweat it out for a day or so."

"You still wanna head to town to talk to Claire?"

"Absolutely." Jo nodded firmly. "Half the town probably believes I stole Claire's sword. Wait until they find out I can't prove my whereabouts last night."

Delta slung an arm around Jo's shoulder. "You sure you didn't steal the sword?"

Jo playfully punched her friend in the arm. "Very funny."

During the ride to town, the women discussed the missing sword and the list of possible suspects, which was focused on the few people who knew about the sword. "We need to ask Claire who knew it existed."

They found an empty parking spot in front of the antique shop. The overhead bell announced their arrival and a harried Claire hurried from the back. "Hey, Jo. Delta."

"Hi, Claire. I called last night and left a message for you," Jo said. "I can't believe someone broke into the shop and stole your sword."

"I can't believe it, either." Claire's face crumpled.

"It can't have gone too far," Jo said. "If we put our heads together, we should be able to come up with a list of suspects. Tell me everything that happened."

"Well, like I said before you left, I was going to take it home with me after I finished working next door at the laundromat. I closed the dry cleaner window at nine, got my banking ready for an after-hours deposit. I came back here to grab the sword."

Jo interrupted. "Did you notice anything unusual when you got here?"

Claire shook her head. "I unlocked the front door and went right to the cabinet to grab the sword. It was gone, so I started looking around, and then I noticed the basement door was busted open. I called the police right away, but whoever broke in was long gone."

"Did the authorities dust for prints?" Delta asked.

"No. It was Sheriff Franklin and another deputy, but not his son, Brian. They took a bunch of pictures, asked questions and then left. In their eyes, I'm sure they view it as a petty theft."

"Except it might not be a petty theft," Jo pointed out. "Which leads me to believe it was someone who suspected the sword might be valuable."

"If I can't get it back, I hope it's a pretty fake," Claire said, "and the thief wasted their time. I have a call in to Sheriff Franklin. After I got here this morning, I discovered something else."

Chapter 5

"I'm missing some antique costume jewelry," Claire said. "It was inside the display case."

"And the sword was tucked underneath the display case," Jo said. "Why would someone steal costume jewelry? Let's suppose one of the other antique dealers was the one who broke in here. They suspected the sword might be worth something and knew exactly where you had placed it."

"I was thinking..." Claire darted to her computer. "It had to be one of the other antique dealers I showed the sword to. It's the same two dealers who rented space for the festival."

She tapped the keys, and the printer next to her began to whir. "This might help us." Claire gave the sheet a quick perusal before handing it to Jo.

The sheet contained two names, business names, addresses, contact information and pricing for rental space.

"Looking back, I was stupid to show the other dealers the sword," Claire said. "I had a hunch it was worth something and they probably did, too."

"Which makes them perfect suspects for the theft." Jo passed the paper to Delta. "It looks like Delta and I need to do some antique shopping."

Claire brightened. "You're good at sleuthing out clues. Ellen's place is over in Smithville and Woody's is in Centerpoint Junction."

"We're on it, but first Jo and I have a couple more errands to tend to." Delta folded the paper into thirds and slid it into her purse. "We better head out. Sounds like we're going to have a busy day."

Claire escorted her friends to the exit. "Have you heard back from Gordon?"

"No. He'll probably call you instead," Jo said. "If he calls, I would hold off on telling him the sword is missing. There's still a chance the authorities will be able to track it down."

"Wouldn't that be something if the sword was worth a pretty penny...and now it's gone." Claire looked glum.

Jo squeezed her arm. "Divine is a small town. I have a feeling the sword hasn't gone far, at least not yet. If the thief suspects it's worth something, they will want to keep it under wraps for the time being."

"You have a point. Not many people sell antique swords."

"But it isn't going to stop Delta and me from paying a visit to the other antique dealers later today," Jo promised.

"Thanks, Jo. You're the best." Claire held the door as they stepped onto the sidewalk. "Hey, Delta. Did you hear the news that Amelia Willis is back in town?"

"Yeah. She nearly sideswiped Jo and me yesterday with her baby blue machine of death,"

Delta joked. "Marlee told me she's in Divine visiting her children. She hinted around she might enter the baking contest."

"If she does, you and Marlee will give her a run for her money," Claire predicted.

"Unless she decides to make her you-know-what."

"Her scrumptious strawberry cake." Claire smacked her lips. "I heard her strawberry cake won last year's state fair baking contest."

"Great," Delta grumbled. "They might as well call off the contest and hand the check and trophy to Amelia."

"Delta Childress," Jo chided. "You don't even know if she's entering the contest."

"I bet Marlee knows," Delta said.

"And we're stopping at the deli next." Jo promised Claire they would report back after they did a little snooping around, and then they strolled down the sidewalk until they reached the deli.

There were only a handful of diners inside. Delta smiled at a few familiar faces as she and Jo made their way to the back. "Knock, knock." She gave the swinging doors a gentle nudge and stepped inside the kitchen.

Marlee stood at the center island, frowning at a pie. She took one look at the women and tossed a kitchen towel on top. "Delta, Jo."

"Working on your contest entry?" Delta reached for the towel.

"Maybe." Marlee lightly smacked her friend's hand. "It depends on whether you're here to spy on me."

"No," Delta shook her head. "Besides, me and my entry should be the least of your concerns."

"I take it you heard Amelia decided to enter the baking contest."

"I figured she would. She's back in town under the premise of visiting family when we both know she plans to win the prize money."

"In a nutshell," Marlee scratched her chin. "It's hard to turn Amelia into a villain, much as I would like to sometimes. She should be here anytime. She placed a to-go order."

Sherry breezed into the kitchen and abruptly stopped. "Jo, Delta. I didn't see you sneak in." She turned to Marlee. "There's a woman out front who said she phoned in a to-go order for a grilled bacon, tomato and cheese sandwich."

"Amelia. I have her order right here." Marlee snatched a bag off the counter and followed Sherry into the dining room.

"Let's go." Delta grasped Jo's hand and dragged her out of the kitchen.

Standing near the cash register was a petite woman, her hair smoothed into a tidy upsweep. She glanced at Marlee and then turned her attention to

Delta. "Delta Childress. I figured I would run into you sooner than later."

"Hello, Amelia. You ran into us earlier, as in yesterday when your big blue bomb came barreling around the corner and nearly sideswiped our vehicle."

Amelia offered Delta a tolerant smile and turned her sharp blue eyes on Jo. "I'm going to guess you're Joanna Pepperdine." She extended a hand. "I've heard a lot about you and your farm."

Jo took her hand, smiling warmly. "And I have heard a lot about you, Amelia."

Amelia lifted a brow. "Good, I hope."

"Just that you're an amazing baker and you plan to enter the baking contest this weekend."

"I figured since I'm here and have some time on my hands, I might as well work on an entry. Of course, I have some stiff competition." She reached for the to-go bag. "Marlee is a top-notch baker. So is

Delta. They're going to give me a run for my money."

Jo took a quick step back making sure she was safely out of Delta's reach. "I heard you make the best strawberry Bundt cake in all of Smith County."

"Is that so?" Amelia grinned widely. "It is my specialty, and I'd be lying if I said I wasn't tossing around the idea of entering the cake."

"I'm onto you, Amelia." Delta wagged her finger at the woman. "Your sweet, innocent smile doesn't fool me for a single second. You came back to Divine for one reason and one reason only."

Jo could see Delta was about to unleash her full Delta-wrath on the unsuspecting woman. Eager to keep the peace, she quickly changed the subject. "You'll have to stop by the farm to check out the mercantile and bakeshop."

"And sample some of Delta's delicious goodies." Amelia winked at Delta; whose face turned fire-engine red.

"My guess is Delta's entry is either her divine white chocolate coconut cookies or her raspberry dream bars." Amelia lifted the bag of food. "I'll see you later."

The trio watched Amelia saunter out of the deli, walking past the large picture window before disappearing from sight.

"Did you hear that?" Delta asked. "I'll bet good money her cake recipe is exactly what she plans to enter."

Sherry crossed the room and joined the women. "Delta...are you okay? Your face is red." She began fanning her with one of the menus.

"I'm fine." Delta waved her away. "Just a little hot under the collar."

"And in the face," Jo quipped.

"Who was that woman?" Sherry asked.

"My competition," Delta said.

"Why do you ask?" Marlee chimed in.

"Because she's been in here a couple of times already today, asking a lot of questions. When she found out I lived at the farm with Delta and Jo, she was asking even more questions."

"What kind of questions?"

"The baked goods we carry, the bakeshop's store hours, stuff like that."

"See? She's spying on us," Delta said.

"That does appear to be the case," Jo wrinkled her nose. "But being nosy isn't a crime."

A customer approached the checkout, and Jo shifted to make room. "We better get going."

Delta and she returned to the other end of Main Street and the SUV. Jo climbed inside and started to reach for her seatbelt when a frantic Claire ran out of the antique shop, motioning wildly.

Jo rolled down the driver's side window.

"Did you get my text?"

"What text?" Jo asked.

"The one I sent you about ten minutes ago."

"I haven't seen it yet." Jo pulled her cell phone from her purse. "We were talking to Amelia and Marlee. What's up? Did the police find the sword and other missing items?"

"No. I just talked to Gordon Rastfield."

Chapter 6

"The sword isn't worth anything," Jo guessed.

"It isn't worth anything...it's worth a small fortune," Claire squealed. "As in over a hundred thousand dollars. Gordon Rastfield told me his dealer friend in Paris is interested in purchasing it. He wants to arrange for a time to come back. There's some sort of special metal tester designed to gauge the sword's authenticity. If it's authentic, he wants to purchase it sight unseen for one hundred and forty thousand dollars."

Jo's jaw dropped. "No kidding. What did you say?"

"I couldn't bring myself to tell him someone stole it. I told him I would have to call him back." Claire's lower lip trembled.

"I'm sorry, Claire," Jo turned to Delta. "We need to pay a visit to those two antique shops ASAP. The longer we wait, the colder the trail gets."

"I agree. We can go now if you want."

"The sooner, the better." Jo promised Claire they would swing back by after visiting the antique shops and backed onto Main Street. "Which one should we go to first?"

Delta unfolded the sheet of paper Claire had given them. "Let's head to Centerpoint Junction Antiques first. It's on the way to the second one in Smithfield."

It didn't take long for the women to reach Centerpoint Junction, which was nearly twice the size of Divine.

The town was off the main interstate, making it a popular stopping point for travelers who needed gas, a quick bite to eat or a hotel stay for the night.

Using Delta's cell phone app to track down the antique shop, they found it in an older section of town several blocks from the highway. Jo parallel parked in front of the store. Delta hopped out first, waiting on the sidewalk for Jo to lock the SUV and join her.

The store was slightly larger than Claire's antique shop. Although it was larger, the smell was the same - a combination of a slightly musty odor, mingled with a pine scent.

There was a noticeable dip in the wood floors, creaking loudly as the women made their way to the back.

At first, the store appeared empty until a man in his forties if Jo had to guess, with black hair and sparse touches of gray at his temples, appeared. "Hello."

"Hello," Jo smiled back. "You have quite a collection of antiques."

"Thank you. Are you in the market for something in particular?"

"I've recently completed my attic book nook and have some empty walls. We thought we would stop by to have a look around and see if there's anything to help me fill the empty spaces."

"Let me know if you have any questions." The man retreated to a desk in the corner and grabbed a newspaper.

"Let's start on this side." Delta perused the shelves while Jo walked behind studying the array of items adorning the store's walls.

They slowly made their way up and down each aisle. After finishing their search, they returned to the back.

"You have a wide array of items for sale, but nothing caught my eye," Jo said. "I was wondering if you have a card or brochure listing your store hours in case I decide to come back."

"I do." The man reached into a small holder on the corner of the desk and handed her a card. "My inventory changes all of the time."

Jo studied the card. "Woody Stroud, Owner, Centerpoint Junction Antiques."

"That's me."

"Is there something in particular you're looking for? I can keep my eyes open," Stroud offered.

"She's going with a medieval theme," Delta blurted out. "You know, suits of armor, shields...swords."

"That's an interesting choice for a book nook."

"I enjoy historical romances...sometimes," Jo said, "and am fascinated by history in general." Her second admission was much closer to the truth.

Stroud reached for a pen. "I'll keep my eyes open. If you want, I'll jot down your name and telephone number in case I run across something."

Jo rattled off her contact information and tucked Stroud's business card in the side pocket of her purse. "Thank you."

The women exited the store and returned to the SUV. Jo consulted the side mirror before pulling onto the street. "It was hard to take it all in. The place was wall to wall merchandise."

"No kidding. I did think it was interesting he didn't bat an eye when I mentioned swords. You'd think he would've told us about Claire's sword."

"True." Jo tapped the steering wheel thoughtfully. "Yeah. You would think he would've at least mentioned it."

"Let's head to the other antique shop. Maybe we'll hit on something there." Delta entered the address for Ellen's Emporium & Oddities in nearby Smithville.

It was a quick trip to the second location, and as they passed through town, Jo thought about her last visit to Smithville, the location of the area's only hospital where she'd visited Gary, who had been admitted after a conk on the head.

The town's business district wasn't nearly as quaint as Centerpoint Junction's downtown area and tracking down the antique shop was trickier.

"Are you sure this is the spot?" Jo shaded her eyes and stared at the front of the ice cream shop.

"Sure as sugar. It's upstairs." Delta pointed to a set of narrow stairs running up the left-hand side of the building.

"I see a sign." Jo pointed to a small sign above the door. "Talk about a hidden location."

The women climbed the stairs to the second story and entered the store through a door at the top. The shop was notably smaller than Claire's place and the other antique shop they'd just visited.

Christmas music filled the store, and Jo took a deep breath savoring the aroma of cinnamon and gingerbread. "Christmas, my favorite time of the year."

"Christmas? We haven't even made it to Thanksgiving yet," Delta said. "I don't know why everyone wants to speed past my favorite holiday."

"I love Thanksgiving too," Jo said. "Speaking of Thanksgiving, we need to do something special to celebrate. This will be some of the women's first real Thanksgiving in years."

"I agree." Delta reached for a silver star-shaped Christmas ornament. "We're gonna have a ball decorating for the holidays. I can already picture the Christmas tree right next to the living room fireplace."

Ellen's store was tidier and more organized than the previous antique shop, and the Christmas-theme carried throughout.

A woman roughly Jo's age greeted them, telling them to let her know if they needed help before returning to a small corner desk.

Jo finished her search of the store and then made her way to the desk in the back, repeating her story about recently adding a book nook and the theme of medieval décor. "You wouldn't happen to carry items with historic antique regency charm, would you?"

The woman gave her an odd look, and then the look vanished. "No. I'm sorry. I don't have anything along those lines."

"I see. Thank you for your time." Jo turned to go when a brightly colored paper tacked to a board behind the woman caught her eye. It was a flyer for the upcoming Divine Fall Festival. "Is the flyer for this year's festival?" Jo pointed to the flyer.

The woman turned. "Yes. Divine's fall festival is one of the largest events in all of Smith County. I'll have a booth of antiques at the downtown antique shop for the duration."

"I think I've met the owner of the store in Divine. Claire..." Jo's voice trailed off.

"Claire Harcourt. Claire has some lovely pieces. She may have something along the lines of what you're searching for."

Jo waited for her to mention the sword, but she didn't. "I'm sorry. I didn't catch your name."

"Ellen Bice. I'm the owner."

"Thank you, Ellen. Perhaps I should visit Claire's." Jo joined Delta, who stood waiting near the door. They carefully made their way down the narrow steps and onto the sidewalk.

"That was odd," Delta glanced behind her.

"Which part?" Jo quipped.

"All of it. She never bothered to offer you her card. Just like the other guy, she never mentioned the sword, and we both know Claire said she showed it to them."

"I agree unless the authorities have already questioned both of them and they know it was stolen." The women climbed back inside the vehicle

84

and headed to Divine and Claire's antique shop. They found Claire alone inside.

"Any luck?" Claire asked when they reached the back.

"Neither one of them had merchandise resembling medieval pieces," Jo said. "Of course, if either of them was the one who stole it, they would know the police are investigating."

"And we specifically asked them about swords," Delta said. "Neither said a peep about your sword."

"You're kidding. How odd." Claire's shoulders slumped. "I guess I better call your friend, Gordon, and give him the bad news."

"Hold off for a day or so," Jo said. "We still have a couple more options. I think an online search of the local antique shops is in order."

"Good idea," Delta said.

"I'll give you a call later." Jo and Delta returned home with Delta heading straight to the kitchen to whip up a plate of sandwiches and warm some soup for lunch while Jo decided to tackle some paperwork.

First up was to order the aprons Kelli had designed. After placing the order, she checked her emails and found a message from Chris Nyles, reminding her to let him know when she'd reached a decision on providing a DNA sample.

Jo stared blankly at Chris's message. Punishing her deceased father and even Miles Parker wouldn't solve anything and to be honest, it wouldn't make her feel any better.

In her heart, she knew it was a petty and childish act. She needed to be the bigger person, ignore Parker's efforts to get under her skin, and put the matter behind her as quickly as possible.

Chris wasn't in, so Jo left a message telling him she was willing to submit samples for the DNA testing. She wandered into the kitchen to help Delta finish making lunch.

The meal was a quick affair with only a couple of the women making it to the table. As was Delta's habit, she fixed sack lunches for the others who were still working and sent them next door with Leah.

Clean up was a breeze, and after Jo finished, she made her way to the mercantile to start her inventory. She had barely started when Chris returned her call. "You're going to go ahead with providing a DNA sample?"

"Yes. The sooner, the better."

"Parker's attorney called this morning. There's a lab not far from Divine that can send someone to you for DNA sampling. They participate in a new rapid DNA program. Parker is willing to pay extra to get the DNA results in hours, not weeks. I think there should be as little inconvenience to you as possible. Would you like me to arrange for someone to come to you?"

"Yes, that would be helpful."

Chris put her on hold and returned to the line a short time later. "The attorney's office is calling the lab. You should be getting a call shortly to schedule an appointment."

Jo thanked him for making the arrangements, and after hanging up, returned to the task at hand. When she received an unknown call, she figured it was the lab and decided to answer. "Joanna Pepperdine speaking."

"This is Dale from Smith County Lab. I'm calling to schedule a DNA testing." The man explained he was in Smithville and could swing by within the hour.

"That was fast." Jo consulted her watch. "Yes, the timing will work."

The man gave her a description of his vehicle and repeated his name before ending the call.

She quickly wrapped up the rest of her inventory and then headed to the front porch to wait for the man's arrival. As promised, he showed up within the hour.

Jo led him into the house and her office. The swab was quick and simple. She watched him place the sample inside a clear container, praying God's will be done.

After showing him out, she returned to her office and stared out the window. The man had told her the other party had already submitted his sample and she might hear back as early as the following afternoon.

In no mood to talk, Jo decided to skip the evening meal, and instead ate alone in her office, claiming she needed to do some catching up. Knowing she couldn't hide out in her office forever, Jo finally emerged.

She could hear the television in the living room and figured Delta was watching Wheel of Fortune. She tiptoed into the room and found her friend remote in hand, her mouth open and softly snoring.

Jo eased the remote from the sleeping woman's hand and turned the television off. Delta never stirred, so she covered her with a crocheted blanket, locked the doors and headed upstairs.

After crawling into bed, Jo tossed and turned all night, with visions of Miles Parker's mocking face taunting her. She also dreamed about her parents. The dreams ended, followed by the recurring nightmare where her mother was finally released from prison.

In the nightmare, Jo stood outside the prison, waiting to pick her mother up. It was the day Jo had hoped and prayed for, had dreamed of...her mother was finally coming home.

She anxiously paced up and down the sidewalk, keeping one eye on the open gate. Finally, her mother emerged and began walking toward Jo, a serene expression on her face.

"Mom." Jo hurried toward her mother, but before reaching her - her mother collapsed on the ground.

"Mom!" Jo screamed as she raced to her mother's side. She fell to her knees, gently shaking her; desperate for her mother to open her eyes, but it was no use. She was gone.

Jo woke drenched in sweat, her heart pounding. With no hope of returning to sleep, she crawled out of bed and headed to the kitchen to start a pot of coffee.

Delta found her sitting at the kitchen table a short time later.

"Rough night?" Delta refilled Jo's empty coffee cup before pouring one for herself and taking the seat across from her.

"Yeah. How did you know?"

"Because you look like crap."

"Thanks for the pep talk." Jo lifted her coffee cup.

"It's gonna be okay."

"I know. No matter what happens. The lab employee seemed confident I would get the results as early as this afternoon."

"Then we're gonna pray about it during breakfast. We're gonna pray about it during lunch, and if there's still no answer, we're gonna pray again tonight."

"Thanks, Delta."

"We're gonna get through this."

"One way or another." Jo eyed the clock. "I better get ready. Your morning help should be here anytime."

"Got Kelli today. Bless her heart, she sure does try, but that girl can burn water."

"But she loves to help you."

"And I love her right back." Delta gave Jo a playful pat on the back. "Now get upstairs and come back down with the Jo I know...Jo the never-give-up fighter."

"I will."

The morning passed quickly, and as Delta promised, they prayed about the test results. Noon arrived with a quick lunch and more prayers. By dinner, Jo was certain they wouldn't have an answer that day, but as they were sitting down to eat, Jo's cell phone began to chirp.

She grabbed it off the table. "It's Chris. He sent a text message, asking me to give him a call."

"Go ahead," Nash said quietly. "We'll wait."

"Thanks." Jo dashed out of the dining room and to her office, where she closed the door.

She paced back and forth, willing herself to remain calm. Her finger's trembled as she dialed Chris's cell phone.

He answered right away. "Hello, Jo."

"Hi, Chris. I take it you have the results from the DNA testing."

"I do."

Jo could hear her own voice. It sounded distant as if echoing outside of her body. "What are the results?"

Chapter 7

There was a long silence on the other end...so long that Chris Nyles didn't have to tell Jo the DNA test results...she already knew down to her very core Miles Parker was her half-brother and they shared the same father.

"Miles was right. The DNA test results came back positive, and he's my half-brother."

"I'm sorry, Jo."

Jo slumped into her office chair. "What if the test results are wrong? Can we have a second set of tests run in case there's an error?"

"I've already requested the results be sent to a second lab, one of the best in Kansas. We should know within a couple of days," Chris said.

"But you're not expecting them to have conflicting results."

"No. The first lab is also top-notch. We've used them in the past for several of our court cases."

"What happens next?" Jo pressed a hand to her forehead. "Should we try to schedule a meeting with Parker and his attorney, to reach some sort of settlement?"

"We could go that route. We could also wait and let them show their hand first." Chris told Jo if he were Parker's attorney, he would try to obtain a rough estimate of her worth. "If they haven't already done so."

"Which wouldn't be hard," Jo said. "I mean, all they have to do is an online search to dig up dirt on my father's death and my mother's incarceration. It was all over the news for months."

"The waters are muddied by the fact the death and settling your parent's estate happened years ago, now mingling your inheritance with the income you've earned."

"Let's say Parker and his lawyer come up with a ballpark figure of what they think I inherited and still have," Jo said. "What will they do next?"

Chris cleared his throat. "My suggestion, and our best bet, is they agree to mediation to reach a settlement. Another option is for them to go ahead and request a lump sum amount."

Chris's words tumbled around in Jo's head...mediation, settlements...leaving Jo's life and those around her in an uproar. "Once again, we wait."

"Unfortunately. I think the best course is to wait for the second DNA test results, which I've already told his lawyer we requested. Once we have the second results, we wait to see what they do."

Jo sucked in a breath and briefly closed her eyes. Her worst nightmare had come true. Miles Parker was already running around town telling people he was going to take her farm.

In her heart, she suspected Parker wanted to pay her father back...and maybe in some twisted way pay her back for what he felt he'd missed out on growing up. Payback was Miles's objective...and Jo was his target.

Chris interrupted her thoughts. "You don't have to agree to anything, Jo. You have enough money to drag this out in the courts for years."

"But the courts could still eventually rule in his favor, and I would have to settle."

"Yes. At the end of the day, he may still be in line for a chunk of your parent's estate." Chris continued discussing some logistics, all of which went right over Jo's head. The call ended with her attorney promising to contact her as soon as he had the second set of results.

Jo set the phone on her desk and stared blankly out the window, trying to put herself in Parker's shoes. Reading between the lines, he was bitter about never knowing his father. Perhaps he was focusing his anger on the only person he could...Jo.

But he couldn't blame Jo. She'd had no idea Parker or his mother even existed. Vengeful or not, there was no way Joanna Pepperdine was going to roll over and hand him half of everything...everything she'd worked so hard to accomplish. The only way Parker was going to take the farm away from her was over her dead body.

*****

Jo decided to skip dinner since she was no longer hungry. Instead, she dove into some bookwork, updating the resident's progress sheets and entering the mercantile inventory she'd worked on earlier.

She finished the projects and began sorting through some emails, which is what Delta found her working on a couple of hours later.

"I figured you were still hiding out in here." Delta let herself in and didn't wait for an invitation before easing onto the chair opposite her friend and boss. "I take it the news wasn't what we'd hoped."

"Not by a long shot. Chris has sent the DNA results to a second lab he's used in the past, but it looks as if Miles Parker and I are related." Jo leaned back in her chair and laughed bitterly. "Who knows? Parker could be the tip of the iceberg, and I may have dozens of half-siblings running around out there I haven't met yet."

"I guess we're back to waiting," Delta said.

"Wait and see what happens." Jo briefly repeated what Chris had told her, that Parker and his attorney could request a hearing, go the mediation route or work out another arrangement.

Delta dusted her hands. "You know my saying...no sense cryin' over spilt milk. If it's true, we'll deal with it the best we can and move on. Speaking of movin' on, I'm heading into town in the morning to help Gary work on the hay maze. Maybe you should ride along with me. It'll do you good to focus on something other than Miles Parker."

"I would love to focus on something else." Jo attempted a smile. "Thanks for the pep talk. I love you, Delta. Thanks for always having my back."

"Right back atcha."

After Delta left, Jo stayed put until she was sure the women had returned to their apartments, the house was empty, and she and Delta were alone.

Jo stopped by the kitchen where her friend had left the light on above the stove. Sitting on top was a plate of food. Tucked under the plate was a folded piece of paper with Jo's name scrawled across the front.

She slowly unfolded the note, tears burning her eyes as she read the words.

Dear Jo,

You are one of the strongest, kindest, most compassionate women we have ever met. You give hope to the hopeless...you see the best in each of us. You believe in us even when we don't believe in ourselves, and we love you.

We promise we are here for you no matter what.

Love,

Delta, Nash, Sherry, Raylene, Kelli, Leah, Michelle and Tara.

The women and Nash had each signed their names, and at the end were a bunch of x's and o's.

A tear trailed down Jo's cheek as she carefully folded the note and tucked it into her front pocket. Hope...that is what Jo needed. She needed hope to ensure she would make it through this tough situation. She clung to the thought that no matter what, God was in control. He had the perfect plan mapped out even if Jo didn't know what it was. She needed to trust Him.

Jo removed the cover on the dish and carried it to the kitchen table. She could hear the echo of the television in the living room, but Delta never appeared.

She finished the food and washed the plate before tiptoeing to the other end of the house. Delta was in her usual spot, sprawled out in the recliner. She looked up when the floor creaked, announcing Jo's presence.

"I found the love note and food." Jo perched on the edge of the sofa. "Thank you."

Delta shifted so she faced her friend. "We're gonna stick together like crazy glue until this mess is over, and then probably for a few decades after that."

"I hope so."

The women made small talk with Delta repeating her plans to join Gary to help set up the hay maze and then she stifled a yawn. "Excuse me. I guess I best head to bed before I spend half the night sleeping in this chair again and can't walk because my back is out of whack." She lowered the footrest after turning off the television. "You gonna be all right?"

"I'll be fine. With all this Miles Parker fiasco, I almost forgot about Claire's missing sword. I planned to do an online search of the local antique shops and pawn shops to see if someone posted the sword for sale."

After Delta turned in, Jo returned to her office to research the other local stores, anywhere she thought might be a place a potential thief would try to sell the sword. She sifted through the sites but there were no swords for sale, at least not in the Smith County area.

Eager to take her mind off her own crisis, Jo began jotting notes about Claire's theft. At the top of the paper, she started with Ellen Bice, the owner of Ellen's Emporium. Next on the list was Woody Stroud, the owner of Centerpoint Antiques.

There was also Jo's friend, Gordon Rastfield. She was almost certain there was no way Gordon was responsible for the stolen sword, but he had known about it and its potential worth.

She reluctantly added his name and then tapped the top of the paper with her pen. Was it possible that Gordon decided to steal the sword after his Paris contact told him it was valuable?

Gordon was a well-known, well-respected antique dealer in many circles. Would he risk his reputation over one sword? Not only that, he would have had to drive all the way back to Divine. Of course, if the sword was worth thousands, perhaps even tens of thousands, it would be worth the trip.

Jo jotted a note to ask Claire if there was anyone else who knew about the sword's existence and then switched the computer off.

Duke, who had kept her company during her research, led the way out of the office. They made a quick stop outside for a bathroom break before heading upstairs.

By the time Jo emerged from the bathroom, Duke was sprawled out and snoring on the end of the bed. She dropped her prayer pillow on the floor and knelt on top of it.

Jo began with a prayer of thanks for all of God's blessings, for the residents, for Delta, Gary and Nash. She thanked him for bringing her to Divine and for the farm.

A Bible verse popped into Jo's head:

"No weapon formed against you shall prosper; and every tongue which rises against you in judgment you shall condemn. This is the heritage of the servants of the Lord, and their righteousness is from Me, says the Lord." Isaiah 54:17 (NKJV)

Jo claimed the verse, and after she finished praying her, heart felt lighter. God had this under control. Now all Jo had to do was trust Him.

*****

Duke and Jo were up early the next morning and began the day with a trip outdoors. There was a clean crispness to the morning air, and the sun was peeking up over the field across the street.

The skies were clear, an indication it was going to be a glorious fall day. Jo lifted both hands above her head, thanking God for the new day. While her pooch inspected the recently planted fall flower beds, Jo meandered to the mailbox to check the mail.

The overhead door to Nash's workshop was already up, and she caught a glimpse of dim light coming from inside. She started to make her way across the driveway to say good morning, but Duke had other ideas as he scrambled up the steps and started to whine.

Jo cast a wistful glance toward the workshop before reluctantly joining her pup on the porch. "You win. It's time to eat."

The dining room's side buffet was already set with an array of baked goods. There were bagels, English muffins, bran muffins and frosted donuts. Along with the baked goods was a large bowl of mixed fruit and on the other side, cold cereal.

The residents and Nash arrived at Delta's designated breakfast hour, filling their plates with food and having a seat at the table while others grabbed food to-go, claiming they wanted to be ready for the morning rush. It was going to be a busy day for all, including Delta and Jo.

The last of the stragglers grabbed a bite to eat, and Jo offered to clean up while Delta got ready for the trip to town.

Nash stayed behind to help, and they made quick work of putting the leftovers away. By the time they finished, Delta still hadn't emerged from her room.

"I hope Delta's all right. I'm going to check on her." Concerned, Jo made her way to the small hall behind the kitchen where Delta's bedroom and bath were located.

She nearly collided with her friend in the hall as she was pulling her bedroom door shut.

"I was beginning to wonder if you were all right."

Delta turned, and a wide grin spread across Jo's face. "What in the world? Who are you and what did you do with Delta?"

"Very funny." Delta lifted her head and marched into the kitchen. "I changed into a clean outfit and fixed my hair."

Nash, who was standing at the kitchen sink, let out a low whistle. "Delta Childress. You're all gussied up and one smokin' hot mama."

"Stop." Delta's face turned bright red. "You make it sound like you've never seen me fix my hair before."

"As a matter of fact, I don't think I have." Jo studied her friend's face. "I like it. The softer bangs accentuate your eyes." She sniffed. "You smell like lilacs."

"Lilac Allure to be exact." Delta frowned. "You don't think the different hairdo and perfume will drive Gary away from me?"

"No way. It brings out your softer, feminine side. You're going to knock his socks off."

"If I wasn't already potentially off the market, I would ask you out myself," Nash declared. "Unfortunately, I believe I'm already spoken for."

It was Jo's turn for the red face. "This conversation is heading south."

"I best get going before I get in trouble," Nash teased. "Tell Gary I'll be there with more bales of hay and to lend a hand within the hour."

"Will do."

"See you lovely ladies later." Nash gave Jo a playful wink and began to whistle as he sauntered out the backdoor.

The women weren't far behind him and climbed into Jo's SUV. According to what Delta and Marlee had told Jo, and what she'd gleaned from the festival flyers, she knew that in addition to the fair, there would be bounce houses, ball pits, a junior sleuth's scavenger hunt, the hay maze and a costume contest for the kids.

For the adults, there would be a senior sleuth's scavenger hunt, a cakewalk, the baking contest, dunk tanks, a cornhole contest and the highlight of the four-day event, a parade.

The city park and adjoining Divine Community Center would be the hub of the fall festivities, and that is where Delta told Jo they were headed.

The community center would also be the location of the baking contest and command center for some of the other events.

When they reached the city park, Jo spied Gary's pickup truck and trailer parked near the pavilion. The bed of the truck and trailer were both stacked high with bales of hay. "Looks like Gary is already working on the maze."

Delta flipped the visor mirror down. "Are you sure I look all right?"

"You look beautiful," Jo said sincerely. "You're beautiful both inside and out."

The women exited the vehicle and began crossing the grassy stretch, past the swing sets and jungle gyms when Delta abruptly stopped in her tracks.

"No way."

Chapter 8

"What is it?" Jo craned her neck.

"Not *what* is it, but *who* is it?" Delta flung her purse over her shoulder and began marching across the grass.

"Wait up." Jo hurried to keep up with her. They reached the edge of the pavilion and that's when she noticed a car parked not far from Gary's pickup...a familiar baby blue Lincoln Continental.

Standing next to Gary was a woman. She leaned in to say something, the tinkle of her laughter echoing throughout the building.

Delta barreled across the cement floor to the other side.

"Delta!" Jo ran after her friend in an effort to head off a potential confrontation, but it was too late.

"Hello, Amelia."

The woman slowly turned. "Delta Childress. Gary and I were just talking about you. Actually, Gary was singing your praises." Amelia's smile never left her face as she turned to Jo. "Joanna Pepperdine."

"Hello again." Jo returned her smile.

"I was telling Gary I must stop by your place to check out your mercantile and Delta's baked goods shop."

"Speaking of baked goods," Delta interrupted. "I heard you're entering the baking contest."

"I am," Amelia nodded. "Marlee Davison told me the two of you are in the midst of a friendly competition to see who can win."

"Yeah. We both entered."

"I figured I might as well toss my hat in the ring. There are a lot of locals who haven't tasted my scrumptious strawberry cake." She turned to Gary, lightly touching his arm. "It was nice to see you again, Gary. Perhaps one day before I leave town we can have coffee over at Marlee's."

Amelia didn't give Gary a chance to reply. She gave them a jaunty wave and walked off, her sensible pumps clicking sharply on the cement floor.

Delta made a move as if she was going to follow, and for a second Jo thought she might have to break up a brawl.

"Let it go," Jo mumbled under her breath.

Gary nervously shifted his feet as he watched Delta shoot daggers at the woman. "I didn't know Amelia was back in town."

"Yes, I'm sure everyone is surprised." Jo attempted to smooth things over and quickly changed the subject. "Delta and I thought we would swing by to see if you needed help with the maze."

"That's mighty kind of you. Wayne Malton is on his way. He offered to help me stack the bales."

"And Nash will be along shortly with more hay," Jo said. "Do you have a layout in mind for the hay maze?"

"Got a drawing right here." Gary's hand trembled as he pulled a crumpled piece of paper from the front pocket of his bib overalls and handed it to Jo. "I figured it's gonna take me about a day to construct the path and at least five wagon loads of hay bales to build it."

"Whew." Jo blew air through thinned lips. "This looks like a big job. I'm sure everyone will love it when you're done." She handed the sketch to Delta. "What can we do to help?"

"Well..." Gary scratched his head. "We still gotta figure out where to put the pumpkin patch and the kid's cow tipping competition."

The trio inspected the pavilion with Delta and Jo throwing out suggestions. Wayne Malton, the owner of Tool Time Hardware store, and Nash arrived with another load of hay.

After a brief meeting, the men got to work placing the bales of hay in position, and within an hour the maze began to take shape. With a clearer picture of Gary's vision, the women began working on the pumpkin patch and children's cow tipping game.

Delta and Jo finished setting up the children's area. Satisfied with the way the maze and displays were taking shape, they decided to swing by Divine Delicatessen to chat with Marlee.

The breakfast crowd was long gone, and the lunch crowd had not yet arrived. They found Marlee, along with Sherry, seated at a table in the back.

"Hey, ladies." Marlee motioned to the empty chairs on either side of her. "Amelia was in here. She said her children convinced her to stay on for the rest of the month. As you already know, she's entering the baking contest."

"With her scrumptious strawberry cake," Delta frowned. "We ran into her talking to Gary at the pavilion. She told us all about it."

"We need to cut Amelia some slack." Marlee cupped her chin with the palm of her hand. "She's lonely, Delta. Life in the retirement home isn't what she thought it was going to be. She misses her family."

"Does that mean she's moving back?"

"Maybe," Marlee shrugged. "Not that I can blame her."

"Me, either," Jo chimed in. "She seems like a nice person, very sweet."

"She is," Delta grudgingly admitted. "I was hoping for once I had a real shot at winning. I already have a place for the plaque on the bakeshop wall."

"I can drop out," Marlee graciously offered.

"No," Jo and Delta said in unison.

"No," Delta firmly shook her head. "If I win, I want to win fair and square. As Jo always likes to remind me, competition is a good thing."

A customer arrived, and Sherry jumped up to take care of her. Marlee waited until she was out of earshot. "Has Sherry talked to you?"

"About what?" Jo asked.

"She's wondering if you're getting ready to give her the boot," Marlee whispered.

"Give her the boot?"

"She thinks now that she's reaching a certain level of independence, it's only a matter of time before she has to leave. She's terrified she'll be out on her own and all alone soon."

"Oh, no. I had no idea." Jo cast Sherry a concerned look. "Thanks for the heads up. I'll talk to her later."

The conversation drifted to Claire's theft. "Have you talked to Claire today?" Marlee asked.

"Not yet. She's our next stop," Delta said. "I wonder if she's heard back from the authorities."

"She hasn't heard back, but she said someone was messing around the laundromat last night. I'll let her tell you what happened."

Another group of diners arrived, and Marlee sprang from her chair. "I better get back to work."

Jo thanked Marlee for the update, and she and Delta headed out, but not before Jo stopped to let Sherry know that Nash would swing by to pick her up when her shift ended.

It was a short walk from the deli to Claire's antique shop. The shop was dark and quiet, and the front door locked.

The women backtracked to the laundromat next door and stepped inside. A young woman was behind the dry cleaner counter. "Can I help you?"

"Yes, we're looking for Claire. The antique shop is closed. We were wondering if she's here."

"She's in the back. I'll go get her." The woman darted to the door directly behind her and disappeared inside. She emerged moments later followed by Claire, who wore a flustered expression on her face.

"Hey, Jo, Delta."

"Hi, Claire. We thought we would stop by to see if you have an update."

"We can talk in private back here." Claire motioned them to the room and then quietly closed the door behind them.

"We didn't mean to bother you. We wondered if you've heard back from the authorities on the missing sword," Jo said.

"No. Not a peep. In fact, I have a call in to Sheriff Franklin and am waiting for him to call me back. I'm sure finding a missing sword isn't at the top of their priority list. Did you get my message?"

Jo shook her head. "No. What message?"

"Some woman from a Chicago area antique shop called me. I didn't recognize the number, so I didn't answer. She left a message, saying she was on her way down here to take a look at the sword. I tried to call her back, to tell her not to bother, but the call went to voice mail. I left a message. I haven't heard back."

"Did she give you her name?"

"Vivian Bane from Elite Auction Services in Chicago. I thought I'd heard the name before, so I decided to check them out." Claire rubbed her thumb and index finger together. "They deal in high-end, priceless antiques."

"She's just gonna show up on your doorstep?" Delta asked. "That's crazy."

"What I find even more interesting is how she even knows about the sword. I still haven't given up on finding it. I did some research yesterday." Jo told her about her tentative search online of both county-wide antique shops as well as pawn shops. "Unfortunately, I didn't find anything."

"I think the sword is long gone," Claire said glumly. "For a second there, I thought my luck had finally changed. I had plans to pay off the mortgage on this place, do a little updating to my home and maybe even take a real vacation after all of these years."

Although Jo knew she had nothing to do with the missing sword, she still felt slightly responsible for the fact it had been stolen. She snapped her fingers. "What about Raylene?"

"Raylene?" Claire asked. "How can she help?"

"Raylene is a former bounty hunter. She has a nose for sniffing stuff out. When I get back to the farm, I'm going to fill her in on what happened. She might have some ideas." Jo pointed to the cluttered desk, stacks of receipts and a half-full coin holder. "You look like you're in the middle of a mess."

"Honey," Claire grimaced as she shook her head. "You took the words right out of my mouth. Believe it or not, the sword is the least of my worries."

Chapter 9

"This." Claire waved her hand over the top of the pile of receipts. "I can't keep up with the antique shop and my laundromat. I'm stretching myself too thin trying to run both businesses at the same time. I'm exhausted and am thinking about selling this place."

"Perhaps you need to hire more help." Jo thought about the young woman who greeted them.

"Kate out front is working full-time as it is." Claire lowered her voice. "She's dependable but a little scatter-brained. I need someone who can manage the dry-cleaning end of my business, taking care of the customer orders and pickups."

Delta nudged Jo. "What about Michelle? She's tidy, meticulous and dependable. She might be a good fit for this place."

"Another employee is needed, but I also need someone who's handy. Seems like every time I turn around, something is breaking. Just this morning one of the coin locks got jammed, and I had to tear the stupid machine apart."

"Michelle likes to tinker and fix things. She's always offering to help Nash out with handyman stuff," Jo said.

"I could use some help like yesterday," Claire said. "Between the antique shop and this place, I'm running myself ragged."

Jo stared at Delta thoughtfully. "The only problem is that we're already running Sherry back and forth to town for her job at the deli. If Michelle takes a job, then we're going to have to start a shuttle service."

"What about the TriTran?" Delta asked. "We could see if they'll swing by the farm."

"No. There has to be another way," Jo said. "Maybe it's time to buy a used vehicle for the women. In the meantime, let me chat with Michelle to see if she's interested."

Jo stood. "We should let you get back to work."

Claire dumped the bin of coins into the bank bag. "I need to get this change deposited." She zipped the bag and led the way out of the cramped office, past Kate, who was still standing behind the counter. "Claire."

"Yes, Kate."

"A woman came in here a few minutes ago, asking if I knew who owned the antique shop next door. I told her you were the owner and that you were here but in a meeting."

"Did she say what she wanted?"

"No. But she's waiting outside for you."

"Thanks." Claire made a beeline for the door with Delta and Jo close behind.

Standing in front of Claire's antique shop was a woman wearing a business suit and studying a cell phone in her hand.

"I'll run your dilemma by Raylene for her sleuthing input and then talk to Michelle about possibly taking a part-time position at the laundromat." Jo and Delta walked to the SUV only a couple of spots away and climbed inside.

Delta reached for her seatbelt. "Poor Claire."

"When it rains, it pours," Jo said. "I can't help but think whoever stole the sword knew about it, and since there were only a few of us who knew it even existed, the list of suspects is small."

"A set of fresh eyes looking at it might help," Delta said.

"Yes, and this will be right up Raylene's alley." Jo consulted the rearview mirror and shifted into reverse.

"Hold up," Delta lifted her hand.

Jo lowered her gaze. Claire was hurrying toward their vehicle. She ran over to the passenger side window, and Delta rolled it down.

"The woman who was waiting for me is the Chicago art dealer." Claire handed Delta a business card. "Vivian Bane, Director of Elite Auction Services in Chicago. Specializing in rare and valuable antiques." Delta passed the card to Jo.

"You know how you were wondering how she heard about the sword? She claims she's an acquaintance of Gordon Rastfield and managing partner with Yves Mercier," Claire said. "Yves contacted her about the sword. I thought you might want to listen in on what she has to say."

"Sure." Jo shut the vehicle off and met Delta and Claire on the sidewalk. The trio joined the woman still standing in front of Claire's shop.

Claire pointed to Jo. "This is Joanna Pepperdine and Delta Childress."

"Claire told me that you know my friend, Gordon Rastfield." Jo waved the woman's business card. "You came here from Chicago?"

"This morning. Yves and I both believe Ms. Harcourt may be in possession of a very rare sword, worth a great deal of money."

"I was in possession." Claire shot Jo a quick glance. "Someone stole it from my shop the day I showed it to Mr. Rastfield," she blurted out.

"It...It's gone?" The woman's arms fell to her sides. "You're kidding."

"I wish I was. I planned to move it to another location while I waited for Mr. Rastfield to get back with me. Before I could move it, someone broke into my antique shop and stole it." Claire hurried on. "I also showed it to a couple of other area antique dealers, and then it went missing."

"I assume you've already contacted the local authorities."

"I have. So far, there's no trace of the sword," Claire said miserably.

"What about the dagger? Was that stolen, as well?" the woman asked.

"Dagger?" Claire shook her head, confused. "There was only a sword. Perhaps we're not discussing the same antique."

"I have a picture of an identical sword. It's on display in a museum in Paris." The woman tapped her cell phone screen and turned it so that it faced Claire. "Is this the sword?"

Claire slipped her reading glasses on. "I believe it is."

"This silver gilt presentation sword is adorned on one side with the king's portrait. Inscribed on the blade is the royal coat of arms."

"Your description sounds accurate," Claire said. "It is a very unique piece."

"Let me give you a bit of the sword's history," Ms. Bane said. "If this piece is the one I believe it is, the royal sword was presented to legendary corsair Alain Porée, Captain of the Corsairs, by a French King; the second was awarded to him in 1730 by Louis XV. Considered an exceptional honor, the presentation sword was only one of four such swords the French monarchs ever presented to a corsair. One of these, awarded to Pierre Anguier in 1745, is currently held in the Musée National de la Marine in Paris, the one Yves Mercier is familiar with, making him an expert."

Jo motioned to the woman. "Wait a minute. You're saying there are only four of these swords in existence?"

Delta's eyes grew wide, and she let out a low whistle. "No kidding."

"No kidding is right," Bane said. "The whereabouts of an identical sword, given to the corsair Duguay-Trouin in 1694, is unknown and presumed lost...until now."

"Well...it's lost again," Claire sighed.

"Forgive my ignorance, but what exactly is a corsair?" Jo asked.

"A corsair, also known as a privateer, was a person commissioned or given permission by the government to attack enemy ships in the sixteenth to eighteenth centuries. These attacks occurred in the southern Mediterranean, to plunder and steal from them," Bane said.

"Sounds like a pirate," Delta joked.

"Pirate is another word used. The French corsair would attack and steal from an enemy ship and bring the plunder back to the crown."

"Fascinating," Jo shifted her feet. "You mentioned a dagger, as well."

"Correct. Ensconced in the main compartment of the case was the sword. Beneath the sword and protective casing was a smaller, jeweled dagger, something the privateer/corsair could keep close at hand."

Claire shook her head. "I don't remember seeing a jeweled dagger, only the sword."

"This is distressing." Ms. Bane rubbed her hand across her brow. "To be so close to locating the missing gilt sword. If I may ask...where did you find the sword?"

"At an estate sale not far from here," Claire said.

"Would you mind taking a drive over there?" Bane asked.

"No. As a matter of fact, I planned to go back there this afternoon. Today is the last day of the estate sale, and you can pick up some decent merchandise dirt cheap on the last day."

"We could go with you," Jo offered. "Delta? Are you up for a trip to an estate sale?"

"As long as you don't go on a shopping spree for your book nook. We got enough stuff to have our own estate sale."

With the matter settled, Claire ran down to Divine Bank to deposit the earnings from the laundromat and drycleaners. On her way back, she stopped by the laundromat to let Kate know she was running an errand and then joined the trio.

"I can drive," Jo offered.

"Actually," Ms. Bane consulted her watch. "I'll follow behind. I want to return to Kansas City before nightfall. I have an early flight back to Chicago in the morning."

Claire climbed in the passenger seat of Jo's SUV while Delta took the back seat. They pulled onto the main road with Vivian Bane following close behind in her rental vehicle.

As Claire had said, the location of the estate sale wasn't far from Divine, but it was down several dirt roads and at the end of a winding driveway.

"How did you find this place?" Jo peered through the front windshield as the SUV jostled along the rutted drive. They twisted and turned until a rambling farmhouse with a long low porch, a big red barn and several outbuildings appeared.

"On the internet," Claire said. "I'm always on the hunt for treasures, and this one piqued my interest. The older the accumulation, the better the chance of striking gold."

"Literally," Delta said. "This place looks like time hasn't touched it in a good centennial."

"I think it's very cool." Jo excitedly shut off the engine and sprang from the vehicle.

Vivian Bane parked behind Jo's SUV and joined the women. "This is where you purchased the sword?"

"Yes, ma'am," Claire nodded.

The women slipped between a row of parked cars. Their first stop was the barn. Inside were farming tools and milking parlor equipment.

Jo wandered to a nearby wall and stared at an array of farming tools, all of which reminded her of horror movie props.

Delta must've been thinking the same thing as she tapped the handle of a set of sharp shears. "I can't decide if that's rust or dried blood."

Jo chuckled. "Could be either one. This wall has the markings of a scary movie."

"I think this place was used as the backdrop." Delta shuddered. "It was where a bunch of teens were cruising the backroads. They got lost and wound up here after running out of gas and were attacked by crazed zombies."

"Or crazed farmers," Jo added.

"Those are sheep shears." Claire slipped in next to Delta. "Not worth much as you can see since they still haven't sold. They'll be lucky if they can give them away."

Vivian Bane, who had followed them into the barn, rubbed the sides of her arms. "Tell me you didn't find the sword inside this horrid dilapidated structure."

"I found it inside the house." Claire motioned them to follow her out of the barn. They crossed the gravel drive and made their way up the front porch steps.

Pressboard bookcases lined both sides of the enclosed porch. Jo meandered off to the side and scanned the shelf of paperback books, crammed full of romance novels.

"Don't even think about adding to your collection," Delta whispered in her ear.

"Romance isn't for me." Jo curled her lip. "I'm more of a mystery reader. I don't have time for romance stories."

"Cuz you got the real thing on the hook," Delta winked.

"Over here." Claire motioned for the women to follow her to a corner shelf. "I found the sword on top of this bookcase."

Bane began poking through what was left of the items, even going as far as shifting the bookcase forward and peering behind it. "Achoo!"

"Gesundheit," Delta said.

"Thank you." Bane rubbed her nose. "I don't recall Gordon or Yves telling me exactly how much you paid for the sword."

"Two hundred and fifty bucks," Claire said. "The owner started out at three hundred. I got her down to two-fifty since I was paying cash and she didn't have to pay the credit card processing fee."

Bane absentmindedly nodded and began slowly walking around the room, her hands clasped behind her back. "How on earth did a French gilt sword make it from France, all the way to a hick town...a farm in the middle of nowhere?"

Jo bristled at the unintended insult. "We may be in the middle of nowhere, but I can assure you Divine is no hick town."

"Darn tootin'," Delta added.

Before Bane could reply, a woman wearing jeans and a button-down jacket joined them. "Hello."

"Hello," Claire said.

The woman lifted a brow. "Say, I remember you. You were here the other day."

"I was."

"I had no idea you were a local antique dealer," the woman said.

"I never told you I was an antique dealer, not that it would have mattered," Claire said.

"You're right. You didn't, but someone who stopped by here Wednesday morning told me who you were."

Chapter 10

"They did?" Claire asked.

"It was another area antique dealer, asking if we had any weaponry for sale."

Jo's heart skipped a beat. "Did you...did you get a name?"

"He left a card. Woody something. I remember the name because I thought it was a unique name for an antique dealer."

"Woody Stroud," Claire said. "Did you have any other weaponry he purchased?"

"No." The woman shook her head. "He specifically asked about the sword you purchased, and he mentioned a dagger."

Vivian Bane cleared her throat. "I'm sorry to eavesdrop, but I know some of the sword's history and the other man, Mr..."

"Stroud," Claire said.

"Mr. Stroud is correct. Along with the sword was a dagger. It was a set."

While the women talked, Jo couldn't help but wonder why an estate sale host wouldn't know about the sword, its value...or potential value. "You knew nothing about the sword before putting it up for sale?"

"I did not. I had no idea it was on the front porch." She shot Claire an accusing look. "By the time I found out about it from Mrs. Clipson, this woman and the sword were long gone."

Claire squared her shoulders. "I found the item shoved on top of a bookcase. I took it to the owner to ask if the item was for sale. She said it was. She gave me a price, I got it down to what I thought was a reasonable offer, and then I purchased it."

"She's an old woman." The estate rep's eyes narrowed. "Mrs. Clipson is not of a sound mind and should never have negotiated the sale of the antique."

"But she's of enough sound mind to hire you to run her estate sale," Jo said quietly.

The woman hissed under her breath. "I'm going to ask you to leave before I call the authorities and report you for trespassing."

"No need to bother." Claire stomped to the porch door and swung it open. "I don't want any of this junk anyway."

Jo and Delta hurried after her while Vivian Bane hung back. She handed the woman her card and whispered something in a low voice that Jo didn't catch.

The trio waited for Bane at the bottom of the steps.

"Who is Woody Stroud?" Bane asked.

"Another local antique dealer," Claire replied. "He owns Centerpoint Antiques."

"I noticed you handed the estate sale host your card," Jo said. "What did you say?"

"I told her if she ever ran across any other antiques to give me a call." Bane tugged on the bottom of her jacket. "If you happen to stumble upon the sword again, don't hesitate to give me a call. Elite Auction Services will make it worth your while."

The woman strode to her vehicle, climbed inside and drove off, never looking back.

"She's a trip," Delta said.

"That's an understatement. I think she would cheat her mother to get her hands on the sword," Jo said. "It does seem a little 'snakey' to go behind your back to ask the woman to contact her."

The trio tromped back to Jo's vehicle.

"I'm beginning to wonder about Gordon Rastfield," Delta said. "It seems like all of the trouble started right after he saw the sword."

"I was thinking the same thing." Jo slid the key in the ignition. "I've known him for years, but it's always been more of a business relationship. I would definitely consider him a suspect."

"Along with Woody Stroud and Ellen Bice," Claire said. "The fact Woody showed up here asking about similar items makes me wonder if he wasn't the one who burglarized my place. He watched me stash the sword under the counter."

"And so did Bice?" Delta asked.

"Yeah, her too."

"So now we have three solid suspects." Jo steered the SUV off to the side to avoid the ruts until they reached the gravel road. "We have Woody Stroud and Ellen Bice, both of whom are local dealers. Although I hate to admit it, Gordon is also a suspect." She tapped the steering wheel thoughtfully. "Putting the pieces together, Gordon contacted Yves Mercier, his French connection, who talked to Gordon and then viewed the photos. He, in turn, contacted Vivian Bane."

"Do you think Yves was trying to cut Gordon out of the deal by having his Chicago partner, Vivian, contact Claire?" Delta asked.

"That's what I'm thinking," Jo said. "Or it could be Gordon was the one who stole the sword, and then told Yves it wasn't worth anything to throw him off. Yves, not buying it, contacted Vivian Bane to get a second opinion."

"It sounds slimy," Claire said.

"Slimy, but we're talking big bucks here," Jo said. "It doesn't take Woody Stroud off the radar. I think it's time to run this whole scenario by Raylene to get her take on it."

*****

"You're telling me Claire purchased this sword for a couple hundred bucks at an estate sale. She brought it back to her antique shop, thinking it might be worth something. She showed it to two other local antique dealers, and then she showed it to you and Delta. You both agreed it might have value, so you forwarded Claire's pictures to your contact in Kansas City," Raylene said.

"Gordon Rastfield," Jo nodded. "My father purchased numerous pieces of artwork during his lifetime. Gordon was good. All of the pieces my father acquired increased in value, so I trusted his opinion."

Raylene studied the pictures. "By the time Gordon calls Claire back, someone has stolen the sword and case."

"Right out from under Claire's nose while she was workin' next door at the laundromat," Delta said. "It had to be one of those three people."

"Out of the blue, Vivian Bane, a Chicago dealer, shows up on Claire's doorstep, inquiring about the sword."

"She didn't know it was missing," Raylene said.

"No." Jo shook her head. "Neither did Gordon Rastfield, unless he was the one who stole it. We haven't told him yet."

"So, this French connection and Vivian Bane, the Chicago dealer, planned to cut Gordon out of the deal, go around him and purchase the sword directly from Claire."

"That's what we thought," Jo said. "*Unless* Gordon attempted to convince Yves the sword had no value, Yves didn't believe him and decided to send someone of his own choosing in for a second opinion."

"Or, Gordon told him the sword had already been sold, him being the one who stole it." Raylene handed Jo her phone.

"The fact Woody Stroud showed up at the estate sale is suspect. He also told the estate sale host about the sword and dagger. What if he swiped the sword and then went back to the sale to see if there were any other pieces?" Jo told her what Bane had said, that there was also a dagger. "Claire insists there was no second piece."

"I think it's time for me to pay a visit to the two antique dealers," Raylene said.

"Except both dealers have already met Delta and me," Jo said. "Which is where you come in. We need to put our thinking caps on and come up with some sort of plan to figure out if Woody Stroud or Ellen Bice are somehow involved in the theft."

The kitchen's backdoor creaked open, and a tentative Michelle hovered in the doorway. When she spotted Delta, Raylene and Jo seated at the table, she took a quick step back. "I'm sorry. I didn't mean to interrupt."

"You're not interrupting." Jo waved her in. "C'mon in."

Raylene pushed her chair back. "It's getting late. Maybe we can head over there tomorrow morning."

"Sounds like a plan," Jo thanked Raylene for her input and waited for her to leave before turning her attention to Michelle. "Thank you for coming by. Let's go to my office where we can chat."

Michelle silently followed Jo out of the kitchen and to her office in the back. She waited for the younger woman to step inside and then closed the office door behind them. "Have a seat."

"Thanks." The young woman perched on the edge of the chair, looking uncomfortable. "I hope I didn't do anything wrong. Nash asked me to check out the mercantile's front porch lights. I'm sorry I wasn't able to fix them."

Jo settled in behind her desk and eyed the nervous woman. "Nash calls you his handywoman in training. He said he recently discovered you have a knack for fixing things."

"I like to figure stuff out." Michelle picked at a piece of lint on her pants. "Someday maybe I would like to own either a cleaning company or a handyman business."

"And you excel at both." Jo reached for the pen on her desk, twirling it between her fingers. "I updated your progress sheet."

"You did?" Michelle swallowed hard and lowered her gaze. "I'm not making much progress, am I?"

"Quite the opposite. I take that back. You're making great progress in some areas and not so much in others."

Michelle lifted her head, and their eyes met. "I am?"

"Yes. You're dependable, hardworking and you take initiative. I've never heard a single peep from the other residents about not getting along. You're near perfect."

"Except."

"Except for your self-confidence." Jo changed the subject and decided to throw out her idea. "You know Claire Harcourt."

"Claire is the lady who owns the antique shop."

"And the laundromat," Jo added. "Claire needs help. She needs help running the laundromat and someone who is handy. Delta and I thought of you."

Michelle's eyes grew wide. "To work in town?"

"Possibly. It would be part-time to start, but first, you will need to interview with Claire to find out if it would be a good fit for both of you. Is it something you think you might be interested in?"

"Yeah. I mean, yes." A troubled look crossed her face. "Would I have to deal with customers?"

"You would, but it wouldn't be any different than working with customers in the bakeshop or mercantile. Claire is looking for someone to handle her dry-cleaning business, taking orders, handling pickups."

"I..." Michelle sank back in her chair. "I'm not much of a people-person."

"But you must learn to deal with others," Jo said. "You can't hide out here at the farm for the rest of your life. I think with a little effort, dealing with the public will be good for your self-confidence."

"But people judge me...judge us here at the farm," Michelle whispered. "They think we're still criminals."

"Some do," Jo agreed, "but not all. This…this is your second chance. I've come to know many of the Divine locals. Most of them are good people, nice people. They'll give you a chance…if you give them a chance."

"I suppose."

Jo threw out a proposition. "Tell you what. Talk to Claire. If it's something you both want to try…give it a day…just one day."

"Just one day," Michelle repeated. "I think I could do it."

"I think you can, too." Jo grinned. "Baby steps, Michelle. Every new goal reached is another step in the right direction."

She walked Michelle to the door and followed her out.

"Thanks, Jo."

"You're welcome."

Delta watched Michelle exit through the back and waited until the screen door slammed. "What did you say to that poor girl? She looked like she was gonna pass out."

"She agreed to talk to Claire about working at the drycleaners."

"Miracles never do cease," Delta teased. "You sure do have a way of convincing those women to step out of their comfort zones."

"Someone has to." Jo patted Delta's shoulder. "And you're not too bad at it yourself."

She hung out in the kitchen to help Delta prepare dinner. Since they'd spent most of the day running the roads and tracking down clues, Delta had decided on a choice of either grilled chicken or grilled steak salads and leftover fruit.

By the time they finished chopping the vegetables, the women and Nash had gathered at the table where Jo announced Michelle had agreed to talk to Claire about taking a part-time job in town.

They joined hands, and each of them said a special prayer for Michelle.

Raylene started. "Dear Lord. Please give Michelle the courage to face new strangers every day."

Sherry was next. "God, I know how fearful Michelle is to meet new people. Please show her not everyone judges those of us who have made mistakes."

"Dear Heavenly Father," Kelli started. "Michelle is one of my closest friends here at the farm. You know she's scared. Please help arm her with your shield and buckler, to deflect any hurtful words that might come her way."

Jo smiled at Kelli's prayer.

Tara was last. "Lord, it's me, Tara. Michelle deserves a chance to try something new and show others she's a great handywoman."

"Amen," the others echoed.

Michelle sheepishly looked around the table. "Thanks, you guys. I feel better already."

Jo, touched by their prayers of encouragement, blinked back sudden tears. God had surely blessed her with a wonderful group of women. "Each of those were awesome prayers, and I'm sure God heard them all."

"From your mouth to God's ears," Delta quipped. "Lord Jesus, make Michelle a mighty warrior and strong."

"Amen," Jo said.

Dinner was a lively event, with Jo and Delta filling the women in on Gary's hay maze and some of the other fall festival activities. Dinner ended, and they lingered over coffee and Delta's peach cobbler.

Raylene hung back after the others left. "That was nice of everyone to pray for Michelle. She's anxious and excited and nervous about working outside the farm."

"More than any of you, she needs to leave the comfort and security of this place," Jo said. "We'll take it one day at a time. It will be up to Claire and her to decide if it's something they want to try."

She changed the subject. "I figure you're sticking around here for a reason. Did you have a chance to mull over the case of the missing sword?"

"I did. I spent the rest of the afternoon doing some online research, researching the list of suspects and the sword. I found a picture of a similar sword for sale online, at least it was along the same lines as the one Claire had. The list price is a hair under two hundred thousand dollars."

Jo's jaw dropped. "Two hundred thousand."

Delta, who had returned to the dining room to wipe the table, abruptly stopped. "That's a lot of antique right there. No wonder the estate sale host was so hot under the collar when the owner sold the sword to Claire."

"If the piece I researched is the same one, there were only four ever made, and one is missing."

"The one Claire purchased," Jo said.

"Yeah. I sent you a link to the site where I found it."

"I'll check it out later. I figured with two top-notch antique dealers showing up on Claire's doorstep within hours of each other she might have something," Jo said. "Is that all?"

"No. There's something else," Raylene said. "It's the timing of the theft. I think I stumbled upon something which might be an important clue."

Chapter 11

"Claire needs all of the help she can get."

"First, I want to scope out her businesses," Raylene said.

"Let me see if I can track her down." Jo grabbed her cell phone and dialed Claire's number.

"Hey, Jo."

"Hey, Claire. Raylene's spent some time going over the information regarding the sword. She's asking if we can run by your businesses. She thinks she may be onto something important."

"By all means. I'm at the antique shop now. If you want, we can meet here."

With a plan in place, Delta, Raylene and Jo headed to town. Daylight had already faded. They drove past the city park and pavilion, where tall stacks of hay lined the perimeter of the open structure.

"Gary's hay maze is taking shape." Jo pointed to the scarecrows adorning the posts. "He even added scarecrows."

From the street, Jo spied the pyramid of pumpkins close to the maze's exit. On the opposite side was a wooden wagon filled with gourds and smaller pumpkins. Miniature bales of hay surrounded the wagon.

"I love fall," Delta said. "Apple cider, cinnamon and sugar pumpkin donuts, the crisp fall air and changing colors of the leaves."

"I'm looking forward to the festival," Raylene said. "It's been years since I've been able to enjoy the change of seasons."

"We should plan a mini color tour. It would be a nice break from the daily grind." Jo warmed to the idea.

"That sounds like fun," Delta said. "We could stop at the main tourist attraction to show it to the gals who haven't seen it yet."

"Yes, we could." Excited at the prospect of an outing, Jo rolled down her window to let in the crisp fall air.

Downtown Divine's Main Street was a hub of activity. Marlee's deli was hopping, and so was Twistee Treat. "I thought the ice cream place was closed for the season." Jo pointed to the ice cream cone-shaped building and a line of customers waiting to order.

"They stay open 'til the fall festival ends and then the owners, the Hillsons, head to Florida for the winter."

The parking spots directly in front of the laundromat and Claire's antique shop were empty. Jo pulled into a spot between the two. They could see someone standing behind the dry cleaner counter. It wasn't Kate, the young woman they'd met earlier.

The woman looked their way, and Jo gave her a quick wave as they walked next door to the antique shop.

Raylene trailed behind, slowing as she studied the laundromat. Delta and Jo waited near the door for her to catch up.

"Already checking it out?" Jo asked.

"Yeah. I wouldn't mind walking the perimeter of the buildings before it gets dark," Raylene said.

"I'll pop in and tell Claire that we're here and what we're doing so she doesn't freak out." Jo reached for the doorknob, but the door was locked. She rapped lightly on the glass pane, and Claire appeared.

She flipped the lock and pushed the door open. "Sorry about that. I've been keeping the doors locked after closing time. You never know when someone might storm in here and rob me."

"Raylene wants to take a look around the outside of your buildings before it gets dark," Jo explained.

"Good idea." Claire patted her pockets. "I've got my keys."

"We should've brought a flashlight with us," Raylene said.

"I have one." Claire darted back inside. She returned carrying a flashlight and pulled the door shut behind her. "Follow me."

She led the women past the antique shop and to a narrow walkway separating the shop from the building next door.

"What's this?" Raylene pointed to the brick building.

"It's empty," Claire said. "Used to be a coffee bar, but the owner couldn't make a go of it. Few people in this small town are willing to pay big bucks for a coffee they can get down at Marlee's place for a fraction of the price."

"It's all about ambiance," Delta pronounced it *ambeeants*. "We don't have the young folks or people willing to part with that kinda cash."

"This is it." Claire pointed to a set of cement stairs and a metal door at the bottom. "Whoever broke in managed to pick the lock."

"Roughly what time do you think the theft occurred?" Raylene asked.

"Right about now...it was getting dark, but not completely."

The women descended the steps.

Raylene knelt on one knee to inspect the door's lock. "Is this a new lock?"

"It is. I tossed the old one in the trash."

"Do you have the key?"

"I do." Claire fumbled with the keys on her ring and handed them to Raylene. "It's this one."

Raylene inserted the key in the lock, giving it a quick twist. She slid the lock from the slot and handed the keys back. "For future reference, combination locks are your best bet."

"Duly noted."

The rusty door creaked loudly as Raylene eased it open. She took a tentative step inside, peering cautiously into the dark room.

"You're gonna need this." Claire thrust the flashlight into her hand.

"Thanks."

Delta shifted away from the door. "You're gonna go inside?"

"I want to retrace the thief's path." Raylene took another step.

"Couldn't we wait to do this during the daytime?" Jo asked.

"Every day we wait, the colder the trail becomes. I have a hunch whoever took the sword is still sitting on it. I believe it's also someone who knew exactly where to find it. I'm hoping maybe they left behind a clue or two."

"The authorities already took a look around down here," Claire said.

"Yes, but they may have missed something," Raylene tightened her grip on the flashlight. "I can go alone if you're scared."

"I'm not scared," Jo said.

"I'm totally Chicken Little on this one." Delta took a step back.

"No, you're not." Jo nudged her forward. With Raylene in the lead, Claire right behind her, Jo next in line and a reluctant Delta bringing up the rear, the women entered the basement.

The air was damp and filled with a musty smell. Jo shivered as she eyed the exposed joists and ductwork overhead. "How old is this building?"

"Older than me," Claire laughed. "You shoulda seen what this place looked like when I bought it. It was ready for the wrecking ball, and I rescued it." She patted a support beam. "Never had much use for the basement even for storage."

There was a trio of wooden shelves tucked in the back. On top was a stack of empty cardboard boxes.

Raylene shined the light in the corner, slowly tracing her way along the perimeter of the walls. "Let's follow the thief's trail. He...or she, sneaked down these steps. They picked the lock and made their way inside. As dark as this is, they would've had to bring some sort of flashlight to see where they were going."

"Right," Claire nodded.

"How do you access the main floor?" Jo asked.

"Over here." Claire crossed the basement floor and pointed to a set of steep wooden steps.

"Hang on." Raylene finished scanning the interior of the basement and then joined Claire, leaving Jo and Delta in the dark pockets.

"Wait for us." Delta scrambled past Jo.

"I have to admit this is a creepy old basement." Jo was the last to climb the interior steps.

They reached the top of the steps and another door. "This door was secured from the inside, but only with a slip bolt lock," Claire explained.

Raylene tested the door giving it a forceful tug before releasing the knob.

"I'm sorry. I should've unlocked it from the other side."

"No problem. We can go back around." Raylene beamed the bright flashlight along the door and stopped when she noticed a scuff mark two-thirds of the way down. "Looks like they kicked it open."

"Sure did. You'll see when we get to the other side."

The women backtracked down the steps and across the basement before climbing the stairs leading to the narrow alley. They waited for Claire to secure the basement door and then returned to the front of the antique shop.

Raylene and the other women followed Claire to a curtained area near the corner of the showroom floor. An open storage area and door were behind the curtain. "This is the door."

She moved off to the side to give Raylene room.

Jo pointed to the splintered wood where the lock had been. "Looks like they busted clean through."

"The cheap slip bolt lock was no match for the force," Claire said. "I planned to install a better lock but never got around to it until this happened."

Raylene tapped the top of the shiny new deadbolt. "This one works double duty with both the deadbolt and locking cylinder."

"That's what Wayne over at the hardware store told me. He said they would have more luck sawing through the door than breaking it down with this deadbolt," Claire sighed. "Although it's a little late now."

"To recap what I know, two days ago, the thief accessed the basement door, crept up these stairs, kicked the door open and walked right to...where?"

"The sword and case were here." Claire returned to the front of the store and the display cabinet. She pointed to an empty spot underneath the cabinet. "I slid the sword and case under here, locked up and then went next door to work."

"How long were you gone?"

Claire tapped her chin thoughtfully. "Well, the antique shop closes at six, and then I run next door to finish the shift at the dry-cleaning drop off/pick up counter." She explained the laundromat was open twenty-four hours a day, but the dry-cleaning window was only open until nine. "We get most customers during the early and late hours, to drop off and then pick up their orders after they get out of work."

"And you do this every day?" Jo prompted.

"Every day, like clockwork."

"I want to check something out." Raylene darted out the front door. Jo caught up with her standing between the laundromat and antique shop. "I thought maybe someone knew Claire's schedule, knew she had closed the antique shop and waited until she was working at the dry cleaner's counter to break in, but maybe not."

She pointed to the picture window of the laundromat where, except for the flashing "open" sign, there was an unobstructed view of the counter. "They could easily see Claire working." Raylene slowly walked to the corner of the laundromat, turned back around and joined Jo.

"The thief had a very specific target," Raylene said. "The fact Claire was right next door when they broke in means they knew they needed to get in and out as quickly as possible. You said some costume jewelry was also missing?"

"It was, but I think it was an afterthought," Jo said. "A theft of opportunity since it was there for the grabbing."

Claire and Delta were still standing near the counter when the women returned inside.

"Well?" Claire asked.

"I initially thought whoever broke in knew your schedule," Raylene said. "But they could've spotted you standing at the dry cleaner counter. Obviously, they knew exactly what they were looking for."

"And where to find it," Jo chimed in.

"Correct."

"Which means it was one of the other area antique dealers," Claire said.

"Or Gordon Rastfield," Jo added. "I hate to say it, but he also watched you place the case under the counter. What if he told us he was leaving but hung around waiting for the store to close and then broke in?"

"I dunno." Claire wrinkled her nose.

"We're not ruling anyone out," Raylene said.

"I'm leanin' toward that Woody guy," Delta said. "He was the one who went to the estate sale and was snoopin' around lookin' for more valuables."

"Motive and opportunity." Jo pressed her palms together. "Motive was knowing the potential value of the sword and opportunity was knowing Claire was next door."

"They stole it right out from under my nose. Something told me I shoulda taken it with me or locked it in my car."

"You didn't know." Jo cast her friend a sympathetic look. "I mean, at that point, we weren't even sure the sword held any value. Don't be too hard on yourself."

Raylene grabbed a pen off the counter. "You locked up here at six, went next door to finish the dry-cleaning shift, which closed at nine. When you returned, you discovered someone had broken in, so there's a three-hour timeframe."

"Right. Stands to reason they were waiting for me, watching me."

Raylene's head shot up. "Do you have surveillance cameras?"

"At the front and rear entrances. They're only activated at night. I never bothered to install them inside the store. I mean, most of this stuff is just stuff."

"One man's junk is another man's treasure," Jo joked.

"Right. The only ones who ever messed around here were kids and only once in a while," Claire said. "The authorities looked at the surveillance tapes, but since the thief came in through the side basement door and never exited through the front or back, there wasn't anything to record."

Raylene tapped the pen on top of the pad. "Do you remember seeing anyone while you were locking up...anyone hanging around or parked out front?"

"No, but the laundromat is open twenty-four hours a day and people are always coming and going."

Raylene took another look around the store with a quick inspection of the back alley before returning to the front.

Claire waited until the women were on the sidewalk to lock the door. "I need to finish covering my shift here." She turned to Jo. "Did you have a chance to ask Michelle if she's interested in a job?"

"I did. She would like to talk to you."

"Great." Claire brightened. "That's the best news I've heard all day." She thanked Raylene for her input, and Raylene promised to do more research before the women returned to the SUV.

They had made it back to the farm and returned inside the house when Jo's cell phone chimed. It was Claire.

"Did you think of something else?"

"No. While we were looking around the shop, I got a message from Deputy Franklin. You're never gonna believe what happened."

Chapter 12

"They caught the thief," Jo guessed.

"No, but they found the sword," Claire squealed. "Can you believe it?"

"Hang on, Claire. I'm going to put you on speaker so Delta and Raylene can hear." Jo switched the phone to speaker. "Deputy Franklin called to tell you he found the sword. How did he find it?"

According to Claire, the deputy told her someone called in about a group of bikers hanging out at the local tourist attraction and thought they might be up to no good. Deputy Franklin and another patrolling deputy drove out there to check it out.

During their conversation with the bikers, Franklin noticed a bulky black case. He thought it looked a lot like the picture I had showed him of my sword case. It was strapped to the back of one of the motorcyclist's backrest. "That's when he found it."

"Strapped to the back of a motorcycle," Jo said.

"A Harley. He told the biker the sword was stolen property."

"How...where?" Jo asked.

"The biker claims he saw it earlier today at a flea market in Centerpoint and purchased it for a couple hundred bucks. He described the vendor, and Franklin is going to look into it."

"That's crazy. Someone went to all of the trouble to break into your store, steal the sword and then sold it at the flea market in Centerpoint? What if the biker was lying?"

"His friends corroborated his story. Franklin checked him out. He's not even from around here. The chances of him randomly breaking into my store, finding a sword case under my counter and stealing it are next to nil."

"What about the dagger?" Delta asked. "Was the dagger in the case with the sword?"

"I don't know. To be honest, I was so excited he found my sword I forgot to ask. Franklin told me I can pick it up at the station in the morning," Claire said.

"That's awesome, Claire." Jo congratulated her friend and then ended the call, but not before promising to bring Michelle by to chat about the potential job the following day. "I guess there's no more mystery to solve."

"I dunno." Raylene crossed her arms and slowly walked to the window. "There's something fishy about this whole recovery. Why would someone risk breaking into Claire's shop, practically right under her nose, steal the sword and then turn around and sell it at a flea market? It doesn't make sense."

"I agree, but people do crazy things."

"It had to be someone who knew of the sword's existence and possible worth." Raylene leaned her hip against the counter. "So why wouldn't they hang onto it, wait until the heat was off and then sell it on the black market instead of settling for pennies on the dollar?"

"I have no idea," Jo shrugged.

After Raylene left, Delta and Jo chatted for a few moments about Claire's good fortune before Jo decided to head outside for some fresh air.

Duke plodded along with her and waited for her to settle onto the porch swing before scrambling onto the seat.

It took a couple of minutes for her pooch to find a comfortable spot, and when he did, he ended up hogging most of the swing with his head resting on her lap. "Make yourself at home."

Jo absentmindedly stroked Duke's head. She thought about Claire's sword, thrilled her friend had recovered the antique. If only she could find such a simple solution to the Miles Parker problem.

Despite going through the motions of a second DNA testing, Jo knew the results would be the same as the first...Parker and she were related.

Next up would be a series of decisions...deciding whether to fight Parker and his claims ...deciding whether to approach the man about mediating a binding agreement...or putting together a package Parker couldn't refuse with one stipulation -he leaves Divine and never contacts her again.

Jo was leaning toward option number three. She would pay Parker and his attorney enough so that Miles Parker would willingly agree to leave the area. And it wasn't like she was overly concerned he could take her farm, although he seemed to enjoy harassing her with the threat.

What bothered her most was that he was running around town, shooting off his mouth and airing her dirty laundry. Jo had worked hard to assure the locals she and the women were good people...good neighbors. It would take only one Miles Parker to cast Jo and the women in a bad light.

She caught a glimpse of a shadowy figure walking past the mercantile. It was Nash.

As if sensing her eyes on him, he glanced in her direction. Nash paused briefly before changing direction and heading her way. He stopped when he reached the bottom steps. "Beautiful evening."

"Yes, it is."

"Do you mind if I join you?"

"Not at all, but you might have trouble convincing Duke to give up his primo spot."

"We'll see about that." Nash lifted Duke's tail and gave him a gentle nudge, to which the pup shot the intruder a look of irritation as he grudgingly made room. "How's the mystery of Claire's missing sword progressing?"

"Believe it or not, Deputy Franklin found the sword while responding to a call out at the centermost point. Someone called in a bunch of bikers who were hanging around. When Franklin got there, he noticed the sword case strapped to the back of one of the motorcycles."

"A biker broke into Claire's place and stole the sword?"

"He claims he and his friends stopped by the flea market in Centerpoint Junction, the biker saw the sword and bought it from a vendor for a couple hundred bucks."

"No kidding. It was a stroke of good luck." Nash nudged the porch floor, and they began to swing. "Any news on Parker?"

"No. My attorney said it might be a couple of days." Jo confessed her fears the results would be the same and shared her thoughts. She shifted, so she was facing him. "Do you think it's foolish of me to try to pay him off in exchange for him leaving me alone...forever?"

"No." Nash shook his head. "Gary said he's heard Parker's name from a couple of the locals while he was in town working on the hay maze. I guess he's making his rounds, telling everyone you're his sister and he plans to move in...lock, stock and barrel."

"In here." Jo motioned toward the farm.

"Yep. He can't take the farm...unless you want him to have it."

"Bite your tongue."

"You're a fighter, Joanna Pepperdine. I have complete faith you'll come through this and Parker will regret the day he ever laid eyes on you."

Despite the seriousness of the situation, Jo laughed. "I could drive him out of town...make him so miserable he can't get away from Divine and me fast enough."

The conversation turned to the festival, with Nash reminding Jo about their Saturday evening date. "I think Gary is planning a special surprise."

"For Delta?" Jo asked.

"For all of you."

"What kind of surprise?"

"I...I shouldn't have said anything," Nash said. "Forget I ever said that."

"Done."

The couple sat in comfortable silence for several long moments, each caught up in their own thoughts before Nash reluctantly stood. "I best get going. Tomorrow is shaping up to be a long day."

"I'm sorry. I'm not the best company," Jo apologized.

"Not true. You're great company." Nash lifted both hands over his head in a long stretch. "I'll see you tomorrow."

"See you tomorrow."

Nash looked as if he was going to say something else but changed his mind. She waited for him to cross the driveway and disappear inside his upstairs apartment.

Moments later, Nash's living room light went on, and Jo slowly stood. "C'mon, Duke. It's time to head inside."

Chapter 13

Michelle and Jo made the trip to Claire's laundromat right after breakfast the following morning. They found Jo's friend standing in front of a washing machine, the coin bin sitting on top of the lid.

She did a double take when she spotted them. "Hey, ladies."

"Hey, Claire." Jo motioned to the coin holder. "Another busted coin container?"

"Unfortunately." Claire ran a frazzled hand through her hair. "I don't have the money to replace all of these washing machines."

Michelle studied the coin box and then shifted her attention to the empty spot where the box belonged.

"What do you think, Michelle?" Jo asked.

"Well." Michelle leaned forward, squinting her eyes as she peered into the empty space. She ran a light finger along the underside. "The metal is bent."

Claire joined Michelle for a closer inspection. "You're right."

"Could I?" Michelle motioned to the coin box Claire was holding.

"Absolutely."

The young woman inspected the box before sliding it back inside the slot. "It's catching." Michelle gave it a firm nudge. "I hate to say it, but it wouldn't take much to compromise the locking mechanism."

Michelle pulled it back out. She inserted the tip of a flathead screwdriver giving it a firm tug. "The locking mechanism needed adjusting. Try it now."

Claire slid the metal box in the empty spot. "You fixed it. Thanks, Michelle."

"It's fixed for now. If someone has been tampering with the coin boxes, there's nothing to stop them from doing it again."

"I may have to do away with a twenty-four hour laundromat if people are going to come in here at night and steal from me."

"As if you don't have enough on your hands," Jo said.

"On a brighter note, I picked the sword up from the sheriff's station this morning. It hasn't left my sight." Claire strode to the dry-cleaner counter and returned carrying a familiar black case. "Kate offered to come in early so I could run up there and get it." She flipped the locks and slowly lifted the lid.

"Whoa." Michelle lifted a brow. "That's a sword all right."

"She's a beaut." Claire ran a light hand over the handle. "I've already contacted Vivian Bane and your friend, Gordon Rastfield, to let them know I'm ready to sell it to the highest bidder."

"That's awesome," Jo said. "I can't believe Deputy Franklin found it."

"Me, either."

The trio finished admiring the valuable antique before Claire closed the lid and reached for the handle. "Let's run next door to my office where we can chat. I'll get someone up front to cover."

Claire made a beeline for the back office and returned with a woman Jo had never met before. She nodded hello and then Claire, Michelle and Jo exited the laundromat, making their way to the antique shop.

Kate, the employee Jo had met previously, was behind the counter.

"Thanks for holding down the fort," Claire said. "We're going to have a quick chat in the back if you don't mind watching the front until we're finished."

"Not at all. I like working here. There's so much to look at."

"Thanks, Kate." Claire turned to go.

"Wait." Kate stopped her. "While you were out this morning, a man came by. He seemed agitated, said something about an antique. I think he was another dealer. He spent a long time looking around like he was looking for something. Then he asked if we had a restroom he could use. I told him 'no' and then he left."

"What did he look like?" Claire asked.

Kate lifted her hand. "He was about this tall, kind of balding on top, and was wearing glasses."

"Are you sure?"

"Yes, ma'am. I mean, he didn't say he was into antiques, but he kept talking about a gilt and some mumbo jumbo I didn't understand."

"Thank you, Kate."

Claire led the way to the back and to her office. She waited for Michelle and Jo to step inside before closing the door behind them. "Kate described Woody Stroud."

"Deputy Franklin needs to take a closer look at him," Jo said. "Speaking of Deputy Franklin, I take it the dagger wasn't in the case?"

"Nope. Never had it, never will, but I'm okay with that." Claire turned to Michelle. "I'm sure Jo told you I'm looking to hire someone to help at the drycleaners. She said not only are you squeaky clean, but you're also Handy Sandy, which you've already demonstrated."

"I'm not much of a people person," Michelle clasped her hands. "But Jo's convinced me it's time for me to step out of my comfort zone."

"It is," Jo agreed.

"I think the laundromat would be the perfect place to take the first step since I'm only looking for part-time help right now." Claire and Michelle discussed the hours and pay. Despite Jo's fear Michelle would tell her 'no,' she told her she was willing to give the job a try for one day to see how it went.

"I'll have Kate train you. Let me check her work schedule." Claire slipped her reading glasses on. She reached inside the top desk drawer, pulled out a scheduling book and flipped it open. "If you could come in around noon on Monday, Kate is working noon until six."

They agreed on the time, and Claire accompanied them out of the office.

"What are you going to do about Woody Stroud?" Jo asked.

"What can I do? There's no way to link him to the theft, and maybe he wasn't responsible. I have a hard time believing he would've risked breaking into my store to steal the sword, only to turn around and sell it at a flea market for a couple hundred bucks."

"True." Jo shrugged. "Well, the good news is it's found. I'll be interested to see who turns out to be the highest bidder for the sword...Gordon or Vivian Bane."

Claire rubbed her hands together. "The sooner I get this sword off my hands and the cash *in* my hands, the better."

Back at the farm, Jo headed into the kitchen where she found Delta standing at the counter working on another round of her raspberry dream bars. "I thought you had your recipe perfected."

"I did until Amelia Willis blew into town." Delta scooped up a handful of crunchy topping and began sprinkling it on top. "I tweaked the recipe a tad and plan to get my highly-qualified taste testers' opinions at dinner."

"I can't wait." Jo dropped her purse in her room and headed to the bakeshop. The store was empty except for Sherry, Kelli and Tara, who were huddled behind the counter, their heads close together.

Kelli was the first to see Jo, and she took a quick step back.

"Is everything all right?"

"Yeah," Kelli swallowed nervously. "We were just..."

"Talking about the work schedule," Tara interrupted. "You know...with the fall festival and all."

"I see." Jo zeroed in on Sherry, who looked guilty as all get out. "Is that true?"

"Partly. We had no idea, Jo," Sherry said. "We're sorry."

"Sorry about what?"

Chapter 14

"There you are." Carrie Ford's voice carried from the mercantile all the way into the baked goods shop.

She waddled toward them, the stretchy skintight leopard jumpsuit clinging to her plump body as she trotted toward Jo and the other women.

"Hello, Carrie." Carrie's strong perfume, something akin to car exhaust fumes, hit Jo full force. The scent caught in her throat, and she began to cough. "I'm sorry. I developed a tickle. How is Mr. Whipple?"

"That cat is such a stinker." Carrie shook her arm, the thick layer of bracelets on her wrist clanging loudly. "He's right in the thick of things when I'm working on my taxidermy. Speaking of taxidermy, we still need to plan our girl's day together. Taxidermy and tea." Carrie laughed at her own joke.

"Clever," Jo said. "I'll have to take a look at my schedule first."

"I planned to stop by yesterday." Carrie twisted to the side, peering behind her in the direction of the mercantile. "When are you going to start running clearance specials?"

"We have clearance sections in both the mercantile and the bakeshop."

"No." Carrie rolled her eyes. "My tongue got twisted. I meant a going-out-of-business clearance sale."

Jo could feel a sudden burning heat rush through her. "I'm not having a going-out-of-business sale."

"You're not?" Carrie blinked rapidly. "I heard you were getting rid of the farm."

"Who...who told you that?" Jo forced her voice to remain calm.

"A man...Miles something. I ran into him at the open house for Craig Grasmeyer's home around the corner from me. His wife finally put the place up for sale. Of course, I had to check it out. Laurie listed it for over four hundred thousand dollars. I hope she gets it." Carrie rattled on about the Grasmeyer property.

Jo interrupted. "You were over at Grasmeyer's open house, you ran into Miles Parker and he told you I was getting rid of the farm."

"He did. Since he's your brother he would know that sort of thing. I was surprised when he told me you two were related. I had no idea you had family in town."

"I don't."

"You're not related?"

"It's a long story," Jo said. "I'm not selling the farm or the bakeshop or the mercantile."

"Oh." Carrie's expression went blank as she attempted to digest the information. "I'm glad to hear you're not selling. I mean, not that I don't think this place is a lot of work, but you seem to love living here and the women..."

"We're not going anywhere," Jo said in a firm voice. "Everything we have on sale is in the back of the mercantile."

"I'll go check it out." Carrie thanked Jo and tottered off.

Jo slowly turned to face the women. "Carrie told you I was closing the farm."

Sherry hung her head. "We never gave a lot of thought to how much work it takes to keep this place going and what a burden our living here is causing you."

Kelli spoke up. "We were talking...we all agreed you don't need to pay us. Our room, board and meals are payment enough."

"Kelli...ladies. You are not a burden. There is no need to feel guilty or apologize. I opened Second Chance because I wanted to." Jo tapped the counter for emphasis. "God opened doors for me that I never thought possible so that I...so that all of us could live here." She paused to give her words time to sink in. "I appreciate your generous offer, but the farm is not having financial difficulties, and I have no intention of selling."

"We didn't mean to upset you," Sherry apologized.

"You didn't upset me, but someone else is getting on my last nerve." Jo assured the women again that she had no plans to sell or move before making her way out of the bakeshop, across the lawn and to the house's back door.

She flung the door open and stormed inside. Delta was still in the kitchen. "You look like you swallowed a firecracker and are fixin' to explode."

"I am, and Miles Parker better hope he's not anywhere near the explosion." Jo briefly told Delta about her conversation with the women and Carrie Ford.

"The man is itchin' to feel the wrath of Joanna Pepperdine. Why in heaven's name would he go around spreading such nonsense?"

"To aggravate me. If he doesn't watch it, I'll drag this whole mess out so long, he won't remember why he came to Divine in the first place."

"That's more like it." Delta nodded approvingly. "I like to see fire in your eyes - as long as it's not directed at me."

Jo's cell phone chirped, and she glanced at the screen. It was Claire. "Hi, Claire."

"Hey, Jo. I'm sorry to bother you."

"No bother. What's up?"

"I was wondering if you've heard from your friend, Gordon Rastfield."

"No. Not a peep."

"Neither have I." There was a moment of silence on the other end. "I'm anxious to get this sword off my hands. I know Gordon wanted to use some special device to test the metal, but I don't know if I can wait that long."

"What about the woman from Chicago, Vivian Bane?" Jo asked.

"She told me she was going to get back with me tomorrow morning with an offer."

"That sounds promising. Would you like me to try to contact Gordon?" Jo asked.

"Could you? That would be wonderful."

"Of course." Jo could hear a hesitation in Claire's voice. "Is everything all right?"

"I didn't want to say anything earlier but I...I think someone followed me home from the laundromat last night. I'm probably being paranoid."

Claire was one of the most sensible, down-to-earth people Jo knew, and if she suspected someone was following her, there was cause for concern. "You don't think someone is still after the sword, do you?"

"I don't know what to think," Claire said. "What if it's Woody Stroud?"

"His name keeps popping up. I think it's time to pay him another visit."

"He rented a space here in my shop for the fall festival and now I'm not sure I want him hanging around."

"Perhaps you should consider returning his money and canceling the deal," Jo suggested. "I can run over to his place with you so the two of you can chat and maybe clear the air."

"Would you?" Claire sounded relieved. "I was thinking the same thing."

The women agreed to meet at Claire's antique shop within the hour. Since Delta was up to her elbows in sugary goodness, Jo headed to the mercantile to track down Raylene.

She found her inside the store helping a customer. Sherry was also still working, and she made her way to the counter. "Hey, Jo. I'm sorry about earlier."

"There's no need to apologize again. It was all a misunderstanding." Jo changed the subject. "How's the job at Marlee's deli going?"

"Great." Sherry smiled, the dimple in her cheek deepening. "Marlee's been having me train some temporary servers for the weekend festivities. She said we should do good on our tips. I'm still banking most of my earnings."

Jo remembered Marlee telling her that Sherry had mentioned she was worried that Jo was ready for her to move out of the farm. "Saving it for someday when you leave?"

"I am. I want to be ready."

"*When* you're ready. I was thinking maybe it's time for us to meet again to go over your progress."

"Right."

Jo leaned in. "I'll never force you to leave, Sherry. When you're ready...we'll both know, and we'll both agree."

Sherry's head shot up, and their eyes met. "We will?"

"We will." Jo nodded firmly.

There was a look of clear relief on the woman's face. She opened her mouth to say something, but before she could, Raylene and the customer joined them.

Jo stepped to the side as the women helped her. After the customer left, she turned to Raylene. "I'm picking Claire up and we're driving to Woody Stroud's antique shop. Delta's got her hands full in the kitchen, so I thought you might like to tag along."

"Yeah, I'll go with you." Raylene shot Sherry a quick glance. "Unless Sherry needs me to stay and help."

"Business has been steady but not crazy. I can handle it and will holler if I need help."

"If you're sure, then I'll go with Jo. Let me go change and check on Curtis." Raylene hurried out of the mercantile.

Jo waited until she was gone before turning to Sherry. "Remember what I said before. Even when you're ready to 'fly the coop,' I would love for you to make Divine your permanent home and will do whatever I can to make the transition as smooth as possible."

"Thanks, Jo."

"You're welcome."

Jo turned to go.

"Jo." Sherry's voice trembled, and she could see sudden tears welling up in the woman's eyes. "I love you."

Jo's eyes began to burn, and she swallowed hard. "I love you too, Sherry." She quickly turned, certain that if she said another word, she would burst into tears.

She stepped onto the porch and sucked in a breath before closing her eyes, praying God would help her get through the next few weeks and would help her make the right decision regarding Miles Parker. The women were counting on her.

Chapter 15

Claire was standing by the curb, clutching the sword case when Raylene and Jo arrived. She waited for Jo to pull into an empty parking spot and then hopped in the backseat. "Thanks for driving."

She placed the case on the seat next to her and pulled the door shut. "I called Woody's antique shop to make sure he would be there before we made the trip."

"Did you mention canceling his rental spot and returning the money?" Jo asked.

"No. I want to be there to see his reaction when I confront him about snooping around my store."

During the drive, Claire repeated her fear that someone had followed her home the previous evening. "Maybe I'm just paranoid." She leaned forward and tapped Raylene on the shoulder. "What's your take on the situation?"

"The most obvious suspect is Woody Stroud." Raylene gazed out the window. "Jo and Delta already scoped out Woody's place the other day."

"We did," Jo confirmed.

"I'm thinking someone should check out Stroud's storage area," Raylene said. "How familiar are you with his store?"

"I've been there a few times," Claire said. "It's an older building, a little larger than my place. The shopping area is in the front, the cash register and a small work area are off to the side."

"What about restrooms or changing rooms?"

"Well..." Claire's brow furrowed. "There's a small restroom. I think it's close to the cash register. I'm not sure about changing rooms."

"If you and Jo can figure out a way to distract Stroud, I'm going to try to sneak into the back to take a quick look around."

"Stroud is sharp," Claire warned. "Not much gets past him. You'll have your work cut out for you."

"He may have surveillance cameras, as well, which means I'll have to watch out for them. I'll definitely need some help to stay off the radar and away from any cameras."

"I have an idea," Jo snapped her fingers. "Leave it to me."

They reached Centerpoint Antiques. The store appeared empty, and there were plenty of parking spots out front.

The women met on the sidewalk, and Claire led the way inside. Woody Stroud stepped from the back. "Hello, Claire."

"Woody," Claire nodded.

"While you chat, I'm going to have a look around." Raylene excused herself, and Jo watched from the corner of her eye as she began making a perimeter sweep of the back of the store.

"What brings you to my neck of the woods?"

"I'm here to chat about the rental spot for the upcoming festival."

"I planned to call you. I'll swing by later today before you close to drop off my items."

"Later today? You were in my shop this morning," Claire said. "Why not drop the items off then?"

"I wasn't at your shop this morning." Stroud shook his head.

Claire lifted a brow. "You mean to tell me you weren't in my store, asking questions and snooping around?"

Stroud snorted. "Snooping around? Why would I do that?"

"That's what I would like to know. Your visit to Clipson's estate sale and telling the estate sale host about the sword stirred up a hornet's nest."

"It's a free country. I figured if you found a rare sword, perhaps there were other items of equal value which may have been overlooked."

Claire couldn't argue the point and, in fact, had pretty much done the same thing. "The sale host accused me of taking advantage of the owner."

"Did you?" Stroud taunted.

"Of course not," Claire snapped. "I purchased the sword fair and square."

"I don't know why you're bringing it up now. The cops stopped by here the other day and told me someone broke into your shop and stole it."

"It's been recovered," Claire said.

"You have the sword?"

"I do."

Stroud peered over Claire's shoulder, and Jo suspected he was wondering what had happened to Raylene. It was time for her to put her distraction into action. She shifted her elbow, knocking an antique picture frame off a nearby shelf. It hit the floor with a dull thud. The frame and glass remained intact.

"Whoops."

Stroud bent down to pick it up as Jo took another swipe at the shelf, this time sending a stained-glass vase flying over the top of Stroud's head. It made a loud cracking sound before shattering and scattering several pieces of glass across the aisle.

"Oh my gosh. I'm Dropsy Debbie today. Let me help you clean up the mess." Jo darted past the store owner, kicking one of the larger pieces with the tip of her shoe. It disappeared under the shelf.

"No." Stroud scrambled to grab it. "Please! Don't help."

"I...I'm so sorry. I'll pay for the broken vase." Jo shifted to the side. Her bulky purse clipped the corner of a rectangular jewelry box. It teetered on the edge of the shelf before falling. A heart-shaped gemstone broke off when it landed next to a chunk of the broken vase.

"Stop!" Stroud waved his arms. "You're a human wrecking ball."

Jo clutched her purse and took a tentative step back. "I...I'll wait over here."

Stroud picked up another large piece of glass. "Don't move. I'm going to get a broom." He hurried down the aisle.

"I'll help," Claire started to follow him.

"Stay there. Both of you." He grabbed a broom and dustpan from behind the counter and returned to the aisle.

"I'll pay for the vase and the jewelry box." Jo reached for the picture frame. "This appears to be undamaged."

"Please...put it down. I'm begging you."

"Fine." Jo set the frame back on the shelf and unzipped her purse. "How much do I owe you?"

"Nothing," Stroud said. "Accidents happen."

"I insist." Jo reached inside and removed her wallet. "Will twenty dollars cover the cost?"

"That's more than enough."

Before Jo could make her way to him, he ran over and snatched the cash from her hand. "I can't believe I'm saying this to a customer, but would you mind waiting by the door?"

Raylene rounded the corner and joined the trio. "What's going on?"

"Klutzy me is making a mess," Jo said.

"I can help." Raylene eased past Jo, and Stroud stopped her. "I have this under control." He turned his attention to Claire. "Did you need anything else?"

"No." Claire couldn't outright accuse Stroud of breaking into her store and stealing the sword. And she was on the fence about him even stealing it considering the sword ended up at a flea market. "I'll be open until six and would prefer you wait until it's close to closing time before bringing your merchandise to my place."

"Before your friend turned into a mini-tornado, I was going to ask you if you knew there was a dagger, a matching piece to your sword," Stroud said. "It's too bad you don't have the complete set. The dagger will fetch a pretty penny, a couple hundred thousand is what I found."

"Did *you* find the dagger?"

Stroud shrugged. "Maybe."

"I knew it." Claire wagged her finger at Stroud. "You went back to the Clipson farm and found the dagger. It's part of a set and belongs with the sword. Name your price."

"I never said I had it."

Infuriated, Claire clenched her jaw and glared at him.

"C'mon." Jo gave her friend's arm a gentle tug. "If he has it, he's not going to sell it to you."

Stroud followed them to the entrance, dustpan and broom in hand. "I'll see you later, Claire."

Claire murmured something unintelligible under her breath and traipsed onto the sidewalk. She waited for Jo to unlock the SUV doors and climbed in the backseat. "I knew I should've gone back to the estate sale to see if there was anything else."

"But you didn't know about the set...about the dagger," Jo reminded her.

"Besides, you don't know if he has it," Raylene pointed out.

"True." Slightly mollified, Claire stared out the window. "I'll bet money he or the estate sale host were the ones who broke into my store."

Jo motioned to Raylene. "Well? Did you find anything while we were distracting Stroud?"

"No. The back was crammed full of stuff. It would take hours to sift through everything," Raylene said. "What about the other antique dealer?"

"Ellen Bice," Jo said. "Her store is in Smithville, not far from here. We could swing by there."

"Why not?" Claire said. "We're already here."

It was a short drive to Ellen's Emporium and Oddities. Despite having visited once before, Jo passed by it a couple of times before Claire pointed it out. "Pull in here."

"I see it now." Jo maneuvered the vehicle into a parallel parking spot, shut the engine off and reached for the door handle.

"Wait." Raylene stopped her. "You mentioned you stopped by here a couple of days ago."

"Delta and I did."

"Maybe I should go it alone this time."

"She's right," Claire said. "Ellen knows me, and she might remember you."

"I won't be long." Raylene sprang from the vehicle and slammed the door before hurrying up the steps.

Claire waited until she was gone. "This is probably all a wild goose chase. I have the sword back. I'll never get my hands on the dagger and should be happy I'll make a tidy profit on what I have."

"Except for the fact you think someone followed you home last night...someone who knows you have the sword," Jo pointed out. "We'll give Raylene a little time to work. She's got a nose for sniffing these things out."

Chapter 16

Raylene stepped inside Ellen's Emporium and Oddities. The smell of the shop reminded her of a combination of her grandmother's rose-scented perfume and Jo's attic book nook.

"Hello." A woman emerged from the back.

"Hello." Raylene smiled. "You have a lot of books in here."

"It's my hobby," the woman said. "I love to read...to learn. Are you searching for a particular book?"

"Not...no." Raylene shook her head. "Actually, I'm looking for a special gift for a friend. Her...I mean, *his* birthday is right around the corner. He's one of those people who has everything, so it has to be unique."

"Does he enjoy reading? I have some rare books, signed by the author, which makes them collectibles."

"Uh...maybe," Raylene said. "He likes to read, but he's also a history buff and collects antique weaponry. You wouldn't happen to have any sort of 'antiquey' items in stock, would you?"

"I rarely carry those types of items. Do you need to purchase the gift today?"

"No, but soon."

The woman tapped her chin. "Now that I think about it, I may have something from one of my sources. Let me take your number, and I'll call you if I have anything."

"Perfect. I'll give you my cell phone number. I left it in the car. I'll be right back." Raylene dashed down the steps and to the SUV.

Jo rolled the window down.

"I need your cell phone."

"Sure." Jo reached into the console and handed her the phone.

"The owner claims she might have a source for antique weaponry and offered to take my number."

"She's probably gonna call me," Claire said.

"Maybe. It's worth a shot." Raylene took the phone. "Thanks. I'll be right back." She returned to the shop and found the woman waiting near the door. She handed Raylene her card. "Let me give you my card."

Raylene studied the front. "Ellen Bice, Ellen's Antiques and Oddities."

"I'm Ellen, the owner. Let's go to the back and I'll take down your information."

Raylene pressed the side button to turn the cell phone on. There was a moment of panic when a screen popped up, asking for the pin number. She pressed the bypass button and let out a sigh of relief when the main screen appeared. "I...uh...I got a new number and don't have it memorized."

"No worries." Ellen smiled. "Just call the store's main number and when it rings through your number will show up." The woman rattled off a set of numbers while Raylene punched them in before hitting send.

The phone on the desk rang, and they both glanced at the screen. Bice grabbed a pen and jotted the number on a scratchpad. "What's your name?"

"My name?" Raylene swallowed hard. "Jo...Joanna."

"Okay, Joanna." The woman placed the pen next to the pad of paper. "Like I said...I may have a lead on an unusual piece or two. They could be somewhat expensive."

"I would still be interested in finding out what you might have," Raylene slid Jo's cell phone into her back pocket. "Since I'm already here, I think I'll look around. Maybe something will catch my eye."

"Of course."

Raylene made her way to the end aisle and slowly walked past a rack filled with period clothing. Next to the rack was an artificial Christmas tree, loaded with whimsical glass ornaments. Beyond the tree was a curio cabinet filled with tinted mason jars and mismatched bottles.

As she walked, Raylene could sense the woman's eyes on her, watching her every move. She turned the corner and moseyed down the center aisle.

The owner slowly trailed behind, describing each of the items Raylene stopped to inspect.

Another customer stepped inside, and Ellen turned her attention to the new arrival.

With the owner distracted, Raylene picked up the pace, quickly scanning the shelves. Her last stop was the display case near the checkout counter.

Inside the case was an array of costume jewelry...rings, earrings, necklaces, cameos. One of the pieces, a sunflower brooch, reminded her of Jo and how much she loved sunflowers.

"Did you find something?"

Startled, Raylene jumped at the sound of Ellen's voice directly behind her. "I was admiring the sunflower brooch. How much is it?"

The woman unlocked the case and reached inside. She pulled out the brooch and flipped the tag over. "Twelve dollars. I've had it for a while. I'll take ten for it."

"Sounds reasonable. I'll go grab some cash. I left my wallet in the car."

"Okay," Ellen Bice shot her a puzzled look.

"I typically don't carry money around. It keeps me from making impulse purchases. I'll be right back." Raylene strode down the aisle, exited the store and returned to Jo's driver's side window. "I'm almost done. I need to borrow ten dollars until we get back to the farm."

Jo fumbled with the clasp on her purse. "You're buying something?"

"It's a surprise."

Jo placed a ten and some change in Raylene's outstretched hand. "Have you found anything of interest?"

"Nope, although the owner is a walking encyclopedia. Thanks for the cash." Raylene darted back up the steps. She returned moments later, waving a small bag before climbing into the passenger seat. "I didn't find a dagger or anything even remotely resembling antique weaponry, but I did find something special."

"Something special?" Claire echoed.

"I found something special for someone special." Raylene folded the top of the bag and reached for her seatbelt. "A little birdie told me someone's birthday is right around the corner."

"Delta the birdie," Jo guessed.

"Maybe. I can't reveal my sources."

"I stopped celebrating birthdays years ago."

"I think you'll be celebrating it this year."

"Leave it to Delta to make a big deal out of something I would rather forget." Jo changed the subject. "Nothing inside the store hit your radar?"

"Nope. When I mentioned I was looking for antique weaponry, Ellen Bice didn't bat an eye."

"And didn't mention Claire's sword, which she knew about," Jo said.

"As far as she knows, it's still missing," Raylene pointed out. "I got the impression she was reluctant to send me to another antique shop. Although toward the end, she said she might have a 'source' for antique weaponry and took your cell phone number. She didn't mention anything specific but did say it might be expensive."

"I'm still leaning toward it being Woody Stroud," Claire said. "Ellen is trying to get your business. She's probably going to try to sell you a hunk of junk."

"Are you saying antiques are junk?" Jo teased.

"Some." Claire sniffed. "Not mine, though. I sell only high-quality items."

"Of course, you do." Jo drove back to Divine and pulled into a spot in front of the laundromat, right next to a Smith County patrol vehicle. "That looks like Deputy Franklin's car."

"It sure does." Claire grabbed the sword and climbed out of the vehicle.

The driver's side door flew open, and Deputy Franklin joined the trio on the sidewalk. "Good afternoon, Claire...ladies."

"Deputy Franklin," Claire said. "You're waiting for me?"

"Yes, ma'am." He motioned to the case. "I see you still have the sword."

"It hasn't left my sight."

"I visited the flea market vendors to see if anyone remembered the vendor who sold the sword but couldn't find anything."

"The flea market vendors are kind of fly-by-nighters," Claire said. "There one day - gone the next."

"They are. The seller could be long gone." The deputy cleared his throat. "I'm here for another reason."

"Other than the sword?" Jo asked.

"It's related to the sword." The deputy nodded to Claire." I need to ask you a few questions about where you purchased the item. The seller contacted our station, complaining you bullied her into selling it at a lower price and claiming it wasn't a legal sale."

"Not legal?" Claire gasped. "I paid good money for this antique."

"Then you won't mind telling me your side of the story." The deputy pulled a notepad from his pocket and flipped it open.

"I'm a regular at estate sales, anything within an easy driving distance. I found the Clipson estate sale online and decided to check it out. I was poking around a shelf on the front porch and discovered the sword and case. There weren't any markings or pricing, so I tracked down the owner and negotiated a purchase price. The estate host was nowhere to be found."

"You didn't approach the representative for the auction house, who was handling the estate sale," the deputy commented.

"No. Like I said, she was MIA, and may I point out it wasn't an issue until said host discovered the sword's possible worth."

"Were you aware the owner suffers from dementia?"

"Dementia?" Claire's jaw dropped. "She seemed fit as a fiddle, although on the elderly side. She's moving to the city to be closer to her children and grandchildren."

Jo stepped closer. "Wait a minute. The estate sale host contacted you to complain Claire coerced the seller into selling the sword to her and she shouldn't have because she wasn't competent to negotiate a price on her own?"

The deputy shifted his feet, and Jo knew she had correctly guessed why he was on Claire's doorstep. "The woman wants the sword back and is stooping to low levels to get her hands on it."

"Then maybe you should take a closer look at the host." Raylene quickly calculated the timeline of events. "Follow me here...Claire goes to the Clipson estate sale Tuesday morning. She purchases the sword from the owner and brings it back here."

Claire picked up. "I showed it to Woody Stroud and Ellen Bice, both of whom are local antique dealers and renting space in my shop for the fall festival. Stroud suspects the sword may have value. He drives from my place to the estate sale and tells the host about the sword. She erroneously believes she was cut out of the deal, so she decides to contact the authorities claiming I took advantage of the elderly seller."

Jo crossed her arms. "I think you need to take a closer look at the person handling the estate sale."

The deputy consulted his notepad. "Dawn Clipson."

"Wait a minute," Claire said. "The host is related to the owner?"

"Perhaps, but it's not particularly relevant," the deputy said. "A crime hasn't been committed, other than the original theft. I promised the estate sale host I would look into the matter, which I have."

"And I'm not selling the sword back," Claire declared. "I bought it at what I thought was a fair price. She sold it at what she thought was a fair price. End of story."

"Not even if the seller gave you your money back?"

"Not even if they walked over a thousand rusty nails to give me my money back," Claire said.

"You're one tough cookie," Jo joked.

"Darn tootin'. I bought the sword fair and square."

Deputy Franklin jotted a few more notes before placing his notepad back inside his pocket. "I won't take up any more of your time, Claire. I don't see how Dawn Clipson or the owner has a legitimate claim."

Jo watched the deputy return to his patrol car. "I'm beginning to think Dawn Clipson may be the person who coordinated the theft of the sword. Think about it. Stroud ran right over there and told her about you and the sword. She decided to come here, perhaps to confront you, and discovered you were working next door."

"There's no way she would turn around and sell it at the flea market," Claire said.

"We need to focus on motive and opportunity," Raylene said. "Woody Stroud knew the layout of the store. He may have even cased the joint Tuesday evening. He knew exactly where the sword was stashed. Think about it...the only other thing stolen was a small amount of costume jewelry. The thief was after the sword."

Jo consulted her watch. "We should head back to the farm. We still have a long day ahead of us. Can I use your restroom?"

"Sure. It's at the end of the hall on the right," Claire said.

"I'll be right back."

Claire waited until Jo was gone. "I suppose you already heard Delta is throwing a birthday bash for Jo at the farm in a few weeks."

"Yes, she is," Raylene whispered. "I don't get out much to shop and have been keeping my eyes peeled for a special gift for Jo. When I saw the sunflower brooch in the antique store today, I couldn't pass it up."

"Sunflower brooch?"

"Yeah. It reminds me of a sunbeam. There's a small pearl in the center, and it has a crystal stem."

Claire's eyes grew wide. "Where is it...the brooch?"

Raylene pulled the small bag from her jacket pocket and handed it to Claire, who unfolded the top and slowly pulled it out of the bag. "No way."

Chapter 17

"Raylene, I think this may be one of the items stolen from my shop." Claire slipped her reading glasses on and turned the piece of jewelry over in her hand.

"I purchased this piece right out of Ellen Bice's display case. She told me she'd been sitting on it for a while and discounted the price to ten dollars."

"Sitting on it for a while?" Claire snorted. "More like a couple of days. This piece is worth thirty bucks all day long."

Raylene wrapped the tissue paper around the brooch and placed it back inside the bag. "Looks like we've figured out who broke into your shop."

"Yes, it does," Claire said grimly. "We may need to turn it over to the authorities as evidence."

Jo returned from the restroom. "I'm ready to go."

"We need to show Jo." Raylene handed the bag to her. "This is what I bought for you at the antique shop."

"It's not my birthday yet."

"I know, but there's a reason I'm showing it to you."

Jo removed the small item from the bag and unwrapped the tissue. "A sunflower brooch. My favorite. I love it, Raylene. How thoughtful. Thank you."

"You're welcome."

"The brooch was one of the items stolen from my store," Claire said.

"You're kidding."

"I'm almost positive. Which means Ellen Bice was the one who broke into this shop, stole the sword and several pieces of costume jewelry. It's time to call Deputy Franklin." Claire reached for the phone.

Jo stopped her. "Wait. How unique is this piece?"

"It's costume jewelry," Claire shrugged. "There may be hundreds or even thousands of identical pieces floating around out there."

"Which means if you call the authorities and they confront Ellen Bice, all she has to do is deny it."

"Jo is right," Raylene said. "If Ellen thinks the authorities are onto her, she'll ditch the rest of what she stole from you and get away with the theft."

"If Ellen is the thief, I still don't understand why she was selling at least one of your stolen items inside her antique shop, yet the sword ended up in the hands of a flea market vendor." Jo rubbed a light hand over the sunflower.

"She's not very smart if she put stolen merchandise on display inside her store," Raylene began to pace. "As far as you know, the dagger is still MIA."

"Correct," Claire said. "I think Woody Stroud was lying. He doesn't have the dagger. Even if Mrs.

Clipson still had it in her possession, once the estate sale host suspected the dagger and sword was valuable, there's no way she would've sold it to Stroud. She would've done exactly what I did and contacted someone who specializes in antiques."

Claire's cell phone rang. "It's Gordon Rastfield." She pressed the talk button. "Claire Harcourt speaking. Yes...Mr. Rastfield. You got my message."

"I see. I did speak with Vivian Bane. In fact, she showed up on my doorstep. No, I haven't sold the sword. It was missing, but it's been recovered." Claire gazed at the case sitting on top of the cabinet. "When? I...yes. I'm here at my antique shop. If not, I'm next door at my laundromat. See you then."

She told him good-bye and waved the phone in the air. "Your friend, Rastfield, is on his way here. He says he's going to make me a substantial offer. I'm going to run next door to let Kate and my other part-timer know I'm expecting an important visitor. I'll be right back." Claire grabbed the case and ran out the door.

"She wasn't kidding when she said she wasn't letting the sword out of her sight," Jo chuckled.

Claire returned moments later, still carrying the case.

"I was thinking," Jo said, "maybe we could set a trap."

"You read my mind," Raylene said. "The dagger is still out there...at least in theory. I say Claire lets it 'slip' to the same group who knew about the sword that she's recovered it and possibly even the dagger."

Jo picked up. "You could lay it on, telling the suspects you think the dagger might be worth even more than the sword."

"We plant a fake here in the store, set up a stakeout and...Voila." Claire waved her arms. "We catch the thief red-handed. And you know what's even better? This plan is perfect. Stroud and Ellen Bice will be here later to drop off their merchandise."

"There is one minor issue," Jo said. "I believe Dawn Clipson is also a suspect. She knew you had the sword the day you purchased it and only hours before it was stolen. We need to put the bug in her ear, too."

"But Rastfield is on his way here to purchase the sword," Raylene said.

"I think I'm gonna go with his offer." Claire ran a light hand over the top of the case. "I'm ready for someone to take it off my hands, literally. It strikes me as snaky the Chicago dealer and Rastfield's French connection went behind Gordon's back to try to purchase the sword, and it doesn't sit well with me."

"You know what?" Jo's eyes lit. "I think you came up with the perfect plan."

"I did?"

"Yes. We're going to make a deal with Gordon."

The door to the antique shop flew open, and Delta whirled inside. "I've been looking for you two. Did you get my message?"

"No." Jo pulled her cell phone from her pocket. "My phone is turned off."

"That must've been me when I borrowed it," Raylene said sheepishly. "Sorry."

"It's okay," Jo turned to Delta. "What's up?"

"I need your assistance over at the community center. It won't take long."

"Now?"

"Yes. Now."

"We'll be back." Jo and Raylene followed Delta to the other side of the street, making their way past the pavilion where Gary and Nash, along with several other locals, were putting the finishing touches on the hay maze.

"Lookin' good, guys," Jo slowed.

"Right back atcha." Nash winked, and Jo could feel her cheeks burn.

"You can flirt with Nash later." Delta grabbed her boss's elbow and dragged her toward the community building.

Raylene, who was trailing behind, picked up the pace as Delta barreled past several workers who were building a pyramid of pumpkins near the center's double doors.

It was the first time Jo had been inside Divine's community center. To the left and not far from the entrance was a small office with a sliding glass window. A stack of folding chairs was in front of the office, with a large open area just beyond.

"Over here." Delta motioned for them to follow her to a row of rectangular folding tables. "I volunteered to help the planning committee set up the placement of the baking contest entries. I need to rearrange the tables to display the desserts. Do you think a straight line is best or should I put the tables in a semi-circle so the judges can walk around both sides?"

"How many entries are there?" Jo asked.

"Twenty. It was twenty-one, but Evelyn McBride had to back out. She's working at the sheriff's department all day and won't have her mile-high lemon chiffon pie ready in time. She's bummed."

"Twenty entries." Jo studied the space. "Let's try a couple of different layouts and go from there."

"Sounds good." Delta grabbed the end of a nearby table, and the women dragged it away from the wall, giving spectators and judges ample room to walk around both sides. They placed a second table adjacent to the first and then paused to inspect their handiwork.

"This will be too long." Raylene placed a hand on her hip. "Why don't we set the tables in a U-shape?"

"A U-shape might work," Delta agreed.

The women moved more tables until they deemed it the perfect arrangement.

"I think this will work," Delta nodded approvingly.

"Glad we could help," Jo dusted her hands. "Let's head back to Claire's place."

"Wait. Not yet." Delta reached into a large bag on the floor and pulled out a handful of numbered flags. "We still need to arrange the placement of the entries."

"Arrange the entries? Wait a minute...I thought you volunteered to help set up the baking contest out of the goodness of your heart." Jo pointed a finger at her friend. "You're trying to pick a primo spot for your raspberry dessert."

"What?" Delta attempted a hurt look. "I'm only trying to help. Volunteering my time is the least I can do."

"Oh, Delta." Jo tsk-tsked.

"Don't, 'Oh, Delta' me. I would never consider taking an unfair advantage. This contest is going to be fair and square."

"So, you'll let me pick the order of the entries?" Jo grabbed one of the flags.

"Are you crazy?" Delta snatched the flag out of Jo's hand. "I figured if someone helped me, no one would question my decisions." She reached into the bag a second time and pulled out a small stack of papers. "These are the names of the contestants and a list of their entries."

Jo scanned the list, noting Marlee's name and her entry…a triple-layer pumpkin cheesecake. The only other name besides Delta's that Jo recognized was Amelia Willis. Her entry was "GiGi's Strawberry Cake."

"Told you Amelia was gonna go for it," Delta grumbled.

"You have just as much chance of winning." Jo passed the list to Raylene. "I would think placement is important."

"Me too," Raylene agreed. "Let's start by putting the flags in the stands."

The trio made quick work of placing the brightly colored flags in the holders.

"Now, for the best part." Delta rubbed her hands together. "This is where you come in. Stand over there."

"Where?" Jo asked.

"Over there. Pretend you're one of the judges walking in here for the first time."

"Seriously?" Jo wrinkled her nose.

"Yes. Seriously."

"Fine." Jo made her way to the entrance and walked toward them.

Delta shook her head. "Where's the fire? You were power walking. Try again, and this time go slooooow."

Jo rolled her eyes. "This is nuts."

"Just humor her," Raylene said.

Jo returned to the doorway and slowly made her way across the room.

"Now...without thinking, where did you look first?" Delta asked.

"I looked at you," Jo said.

Delta threw her hands in the air. "Not me. At the table."

"I'll do it." Raylene jogged to the entrance and began making her way back. She stopped when she reached the first table on the right and tapped the top. "I looked right here."

"Front and center. That makes sense." Delta began humming as she grabbed the number seven flag and placed it at the end of the table. "My lucky number seven. While I do this, I need someone to sketch out a diagram." She grabbed a large roll of clear plastic tape from the bag.

"What are you doing?" Jo asked.

"Taping the flags to the table. I'm sure some of the other contestants will swing by and check it out ahead of time. I don't want them getting any funny ideas."

"What sort of funny ideas?"

"Like switching the numbers around and trying to steal my spot." Delta peeled off a large piece of tape and pressed the sticky side on the base of the placeholder and the table. She took a step back. "There. That should do it."

Jo playfully pressed a hand to her friend's forehead. "I think you're overheated and spending too much time in a hot kitchen."

"I am not." Delta smacked her hand away. "This is serious stuff. We've determined a decent viewing spot is the first one at the end. Now let's figure out the most obscure spot...a location where someone's entry might not get as much attention as some of the others."

"You mean Amelia's entry?" Jo asked.

"In the corner," Raylene said. "Far left corner pocket."

Delta hurried to the corner and placed the number six near the back and reached for the tape.

"Hold up," Jo stopped her. "Don't you want to put the numbers in order?"

"Placing the numbers in order would make the most sense," Delta agreed. "I don't want the other contestants to think I'm playing favorites and giving anyone special consideration."

"As in picking a prime spot?" Jo grinned.

"Forget numbering in order." Delta waved dismissively. "Jackie put me in charge of setting up the tables, so I'm going to do it my way. My lucky number seven is going to stay right where it is, and

Amelia's number six is going right here." She set the numbered flag on the corner and repeated the process of taping the base to the table.

"One more layer of tape." Delta slapped another layer of tape on top and pressed down as she smoothed the edges. "That oughta do it."

Raylene pressed down on the base. "You're going to need a chainsaw to saw that one off."

"A little extra tape isn't gonna hurt anybody. Besides, we don't want to risk someone coming along and bumping it." Delta straightened her back to inspect her handiwork. "Now for the rest."

They made quick work of positioning the rest of the numbered flags. Marlee, who was number eighteen, was only two desserts down from Delta.

"You gave Marlee a decent spot." Jo finished her sketch and handed it to Delta, who promptly taped it to the front of the tables.

"I'll send a copy of the layout to Jackie to forward to the other contestants." Delta dropped the roll of tape in the bag and led the way to the exit. "You guys have any luck figuring out who stole Claire's sword?"

"No, but I think we're getting close," Jo said. "We're going to set a trap to hopefully lure the thief back this evening."

"What if you set the trap and they don't show up?" Delta held the door.

"We'll cross that bridge when we get to it. Where are you headed?"

"Home. I'm assembling my last round of ingredients for my raspberry dessert. I've decided I'm not going to make it until first thing tomorrow morning. The judging doesn't start until one, which will give me plenty of time to whip up my winning recipe. Fresh is best."

"Fresh is best," Jo repeated. "We'll be home a little later. We're waiting for Gordon Rastfield. He finally called Claire back and is on his way here to present her with a substantial offer for the sword."

"What about that other woman...Vivian something?"

"Claire's decided she didn't appreciate the woman's sneaky, underhanded tactic to cut Gordon out."

"I don't blame her," Delta said. "You should never trust people who connive for an unfair advantage."

"Like picking a primo spot for a baking contest entry," Jo reminded her.

"No. Maybe I picked the worst spot," Delta argued. "Mine is first seen and first forgotten by the time the judges get to the end."

After Delta left, Raylene and Jo stopped to chat with Nash and Gary before making their way back to Claire's antique shop. She spied Claire and a familiar figure standing near the front window. Her friend was clutching the sword case, an anxious expression on her face.

"Uh-oh," Jo said. "This can't be good."

Chapter 18

Dawn Clipson stood with her back to Jo and Raylene. She never turned as Jo eased the door open and followed Raylene inside. "I've contacted the local authorities."

"And I've already spoken with them," Claire replied in a tight voice. "They cleared me of any wrongdoing. I purchased this sword and am now the rightful owner."

"My mother has dementia. She had no idea she was selling the sword," the woman insisted. "You took advantage of an elderly person."

"I did not. Mrs. Clipson and I had a nice discussion about the piece. She remembered a great many details about how her husband acquired it after the death of a friend. She said she never cared for it and had forgotten it was on the porch shelf."

"Had she known its value; she never would've sold it for pennies."

"I didn't know the value, either. In fact, I'm still not one hundred percent certain of how much it's actually worth."

"But you know it's worth far more than what you paid for it." The woman reached for her wallet. "I'm willing to pay you double what you paid my client. I'll give you five hundred dollars right now."

"No." Claire shook her head.

"Six hundred."

"Uh-uh."

"Seven fifty and that's my final offer."

Claire tightened her grip on the case. "I am not selling this sword for seven hundred and fifty dollars. I'm sorry if you believe I took advantage of your client, but I can assure you I did not. I already have a buyer lined up, and the sword will be gone tomorrow."

"Tomorrow? You can't sell the sword. You're not the rightful owner." The woman glared at Claire. "You haven't heard the last of this."

Dawn Clipson abruptly turned on her heel, a dark look on her face as she stormed out of the shop. The door slammed behind her, and Jo jumped. "That went well."

"It went over like a lead balloon." Claire briefly closed her eyes. "I can't say as I blame her for being upset. Reading between the lines, she didn't even know of the sword's existence until Woody Stroud showed up and started asking questions."

"Looks like we can skip the plan to let Clipson know the sword is being sold," Jo said. "One down, two more to go."

"What time are Woody Stroud and Ellen Bice stopping by to drop off their merchandise?" Raylene asked.

"I told them not to come until after five, so we have a couple of hours." Claire consulted her watch. "Gordon should be here shortly."

The women chatted about the details of their plan to catch the thief, and then Claire asked what Delta had needed earlier.

Jo briefly told her about Delta's offer to help with the baking contest, the table layout and her detailed arrangement of each contestant's dish.

"She taped the flags to the table?" Claire shook her head. "Amelia Willis sure has upset Delta's applecart."

Jo caught a glimpse of a man striding past the store's front window. "It looks like Gordon is here."

Gordon Rastfield stepped inside the store, approaching Jo first as he gave her a quick hug. "It's good to see you again." He released his grip. "I heard another dealer, Vivian Bane, showed up unexpectedly trying to get her hands on the sword."

"She's not the only one," Claire muttered.

"And I'm sure she told you what Yves Mercer told me, that there was also a dagger."

"She did. I'm certain the owner of the estate, who caught wind of the sword's value, has probably torn her place apart looking for it."

"I see you're keeping the sword safe." Gordon pointed to the black case.

"Barely. This thing has made its rounds and caused me my fair share of aggravation." Claire opened the case and turned it so Gordon could inspect the contents. "I'm ready for it to leave for good."

"May I?" Gordon motioned to the sword.

"Of course."

"I planned to bring the special metal tester, but after additional research, I decided it wasn't necessary." He carefully removed the antique from the case and slowly turned it over in his hands. "This is a rare piece...one of only four in existence and until this week, its whereabouts unknown."

Gordon's eyes narrowed. "Where did you say you found it?"

"An estate sale...an old farm outside of town. I try to make it to most of the sales in the area." Claire explained how she'd been poking around the front porch and noticed the case sitting on top of a bookcase. "I took one look at it and figured at the very least, it was a unique piece."

"Out of curiosity, how much did you pay for it?"

"Does it matter?" Claire asked. "I don't mean that in a rude way, but does it affect your offer?"

"Not in the least. My offer is one hundred and ninety thousand dollars."

Jo's mouth fell open.

"Holy cannoli." Raylene let out a low whistle. "I wish I had been the one to find it."

"I..." Claire blinked rapidly as she digested Gordon's offer. "One hundred and ninety thousand dollars."

"Yes, and if the dagger had been with the sword, I could have doubled the purchase price."

Claire swayed slightly, and Jo wondered if she was going to hit the floor. She reached out to steady herself. "I'll take it."

"I thought you would." Gordon carefully placed the sword back in the case before reaching inside his jacket and pulling out a leather embossed check case. "Who should I make the check out to?"

"Claire Harcourt. Claire with an 'I' and H-A-R-C-O-U-R-T."

Gordon finished writing the check. He ripped it off and handed it to her. "I believe once in every antique dealer's lifetime, they stumble upon a real gem. Sometimes it happens twice. Today is your lucky day."

Claire's hand trembled as she gazed at the check, and she let out a loud "whoop."

"Dinner is on you," Jo joked.

"You betcha." Claire waved the check in the air, eyeing her friend. "Are you sure I can trust this check won't bounce?"

"I can assure you it will clear the bank. We can place a quick call to my banker if it would ease your mind."

"He's good for it," Jo assured her.

Gordon snapped the latches on the case and picked it up. "I have a meeting this evening and need to get going." He turned to Jo. "It was so nice to see you again under more pleasant circumstances."

"It's nice to see you again, too," Jo smiled warmly. "If I'm ever in the market for fine art or antiques, I'll be sure to look you up."

He spun on his heel and Raylene reached out to stop him. "Hang on. Would it be possible for you to take the sword out the back door?"

"The back?"

"Raylene is right. I would like to keep the sale of the sword a secret, at least for a day or so," Claire explained.

"I'll need to bring my car around back." Gordon handed the case to Jo.

"Continue to the stop sign at the end of the street. Turn right, and you'll see an alley that runs along the back. We'll meet you there."

Jo waited for Gordon to exit the store. "Smart thinking, Raylene. He would've walked right out of here in broad daylight, carrying the case and potentially undermining our sting."

"Yeah, thanks for thinking ahead." Claire took the case from Jo, and the trio headed down the hall to the rear exit.

Gordon was already there waiting near the back of his car. "It was a pleasure doing business. Keep me in mind if you ever run across anything else you suspect might be worth something."

"Absolutely," Claire promised. "Who knows? Maybe the dagger will surface. You can be certain of one thing. I'll be on the lookout."

The women watched Gordon place the case inside his car and drive off.

"I was serious about dinner," Claire said. "We can celebrate down at Marlee's after I meet with Ellen Bice and Woody Stroud."

"Which means we need to get out of here," Jo said.

"Right." Claire gave them a thumbs up. "I've been rehearsing what I'm going to say to them." She repeated what she had already told Dawn Clipson. She had a buyer who would be picking the sword up in the morning, and it wasn't leaving her sight. "I might even embellish to make it almost too good for the thief to resist trying again."

"You told Stroud the sword was recovered, but what about Ellen Bice?" Jo asked. "I'm sure the authorities questioned her after the theft, and she still believes the sword is gone."

"True." Claire tapped her chin thoughtfully. "I'll make sure she knows the sword was recovered and tell her the buyer is picking it up tomorrow morning."

"You'll have to make sure you stress the buyer will be here first thing in the morning, so they'll feel the pressure to make a move tonight."

"I don't think setting up a sting here makes sense." Raylene spun in a slow circle. "There's no way anyone is going to believe Claire would be dumb enough to leave it here to be stolen a second time, plus she's going to tell them the sword isn't leaving her sight."

"She's right," Claire said. "I would be a fool to leave it here."

"So, the sting moves to your place," Jo said. "We know it's one of three people...Dawn Clipson, Woody Stroud or Ellen Bice. Now it's a matter of waiting to see which one shows up."

Chapter 19

After Jo and Raylene left, Claire puttered around inside her antique shop, making sure the spaces Ellen Bice and Woody Stroud had rented were clean and empty.

She mulled over the sale of the sword, having second thoughts that maybe she shouldn't have been so quick to sell it to Gordon Rastfield. What if Vivian Bane had offered her even more?

Claire reminded herself of the underhanded way in which Bane and the dealer from France had tried to cut Jo's friend out of the deal. It was too late now - the sword was long gone, and she had a check in her hand.

Woody Stroud was the first to arrive. Claire heard him before she saw him as he banged into the entrance door, rattling the glass pane.

She hurried to help him maneuver a metal cart through the narrow doorway. "Good heavens, Woody. Do you think you'll have room for all of this stuff?"

"I'll make room. Where there's a will, there's a way." Woody shifted the cart to the right and lifted the bottom as it clattered across the threshold. "I couldn't decide on a theme, so I brought a little of everything."

"I can see if I have some extra room," Claire said. "Is this all of it?"

"Nope." Stroud shook his head. "My trunk is full."

"Now I know it won't all fit." Claire led him to the empty shelves. He began unloading his cart while she cleared another spot and then returned to check on his progress.

Woody placed a petite crystal lamp on the top shelf. "Are you still in the market to sell the sword? I might have a buyer."

"Actually, I already have it sold to a reputable dealer in Kansas City."

"Oh." Woody's face fell. "I'm sorry to hear that, and I'm sorry about earlier. All of this moving merchandise has me stressed out."

"It's okay. I'm sorry, too. The festival is fun but a lot of work." Claire pushed a stray strand of hair from her eyes. "Now if I can make it through tonight without someone trying to steal the sword and the other piece."

Woody's head snapped back. "What other piece?"

"The one I'm keeping under wraps until the buyer shows up first thing tomorrow morning. I don't plan to let either of them out of my sight."

"Would you mind showing me what else you have?" Woody rubbed his hands together.

Claire led him across the room to the counter and a small wooden box sitting on top. "I'm not going to jinx myself this time by showing it to anyone, but I can say I'm quite certain I'll be able to sell it for a nice chunk of change."

Despite Woody's best attempts to convince Claire to show him what else she had, she politely refused. "I plan to take both pieces home for safekeeping."

Woody gave up trying to convince Claire and finished unloading his items. He was packing up when Ellen Bice arrived with her merchandise.

Claire waited for Woody to leave and then told Ellen she'd recovered the sword, and as luck would have it, she'd also managed to get her hands on another item of potential value.

Like Woody, Ellen attempted to convince Claire to sell the items to her interested party, and Claire had to wonder if Woody's contact and Ellen's contact was the same person...maybe it was Vivian Bane.

She remembered the sunflower brooch Raylene had purchased from Ellen. Claire repeated how she believed she had both items sold for top dollar and planned to take them home with her that evening.

Ellen moved at a snail's pace, cramming her sale items onto every square inch of her rented space. Finally, the woman finished rearranging her items and left.

Claire carried the smaller box with her out of the store, stopping by the laundromat to let Kate and her other part-timer, Bonnie, know she would be down the street at Marlee's. She promised to return later to lock up before heading home.

*****

While Claire was setting the stage for the setup, Jo made sure she kept her cell phone handy in case she called.

With time to kill before meeting Claire at Marlee's deli, Raylene and Jo decided to stop by the hay maze to check on Gary and Nash, who were finishing up.

"You're just in time," Nash said. "We need someone to give it a test run."

"I'm game," Raylene clapped her hands. "I've never been inside a hay maze."

"Let's give it a go." Jo propelled her forward as they made their way to the entrance. The interior of the maze was taller than it appeared from the outside, surrounding them with towering stacks of hay bales.

The women walked to the first turn and slowed when they reached the corner. Dangling from the square bales were thick spider webs filled with furry black spiders who peered down at them as if daring them to come closer.

Raylene curled her lip. "I hate spiders."

"Me too."

The women rounded the corner, choosing a path to the left where they hit their first dead end.

"We came from that way." Jo pointed to the right.

"No, I'm pretty sure we came in from the left," Raylene said.

"My sense of direction is questionable," Jo joked. "Left it is."

The women veered to the left, turned another corner...and hit another dead end.

"It looks like you were right," Raylene said.

The duo wove their way through the maze, backtracking as often as they moved forward.

"I have an idea." Raylene pointed to the ceiling. "All we need to do is follow along with the ceiling. The exit is over there."

Certain they were finally heading in the right direction, they picked up the pace, rounded another bend and hit another dead end.

They backtracked once again until they spied a familiar set of jack-o'-lanterns perched atop a hay bale.

"I'm pretty sure we're going in circles," Raylene giggled.

"We may never get out of here. How long did Nash and Gary tell us this was supposed to take?"

"An hour," Raylene patted her stomach. "All of this walking in circles is making me hungry."

It was another half an hour before the women consulted the pavilion ceiling again and realized they were close to the exit.

"I think we're almost there," Jo said excitedly.

"You're right." The women turned left and then right. Overhead was a bright orange and black sign that read, "Jumpin' Jack-o'-lanterns! You made it!"

Ahhh!

A woman's bloodcurdling scream filled the air. The scream was followed by the clanking of heavy chains being dragged across a wooden floor.

Jo stumbled backward, colliding with Raylene and stepping on her toe. "Oh my gosh."

Nash, who was standing near the exit, burst out laughing as he pointed at a speaker directly overhead. "The maze ends with a bang."

"You scared me half to death." Jo marched across the floor and playfully punched him in the arm.

"That's the point," Gary grinned. "It's supposed to be scary."

"I caught it all on my phone." Nash switched his cell phone on, and the women watched as they exited the maze.

Ahhh. Startled, Jo jumped back at the woman's shrill scream and collided with Raylene, knocking her off balance.

"You got me good," Jo chuckled. "You need to get Delta, too."

"She'll murder Gary and Nash," Raylene laughed.

"Nah." Jo waved dismissively. "She might get mad for a minute, but she'll get over it. I loved the maze."

"Me too. You guys did a great job."

"Was it tricky?" Gary asked.

"Tricky? We got lost so many times," Raylene shook her head. "I think you'll end up rescuing a few people."

Jo pointed to a nearby wagon, the back half stacked with bales of hay. "Are you planning to use those for something else?"

Gary and Nash exchanged a quick glance. "Those are some leftovers," Nash said. "Gary has plans for them. Speaking of plans, it's time to head home for dinner."

"Claire is buying Raylene and me dinner," Jo said. "We're working on a special…"

"Project," Raylene interrupted. "Claire sold her sword, and she wants to treat us to dinner at Marlee's deli."

"Have you told Delta?" Nash asked.

"No. I need to give her a heads up." Jo removed her cell phone from her back pocket and switched it on. She dialed the house phone, and Delta picked up. "Second Chance. Delta speaking."

"Hey, Delta. It's me, Jo. We finished a test run of Gary and Nash's amazing maze and are heading over to Marlee's for dinner. Claire is treating us to celebrate selling the sword."

"Oh, good. Claire's finally got that thing off her hands. Tell her I said congratulations."

"Ask her what we're having for dinner?" Gary whispered.

"Gary wants to know what you're having for dinner."

"Pot roast with red potatoes, cooked carrots and a side salad."

Jo repeated what Delta had said, and Gary licked his lips. "I'm on my way."

"Gary's bringing his appetite," Jo said.

"Good. Thanks for letting me know about dinner."

"You're welcome." Jo slid the phone back into her pocket after ending the call. "We're missing out on Delta's delicious pot roast."

"But there's Marlee's pastrami on rye," Raylene said. "Maybe Delta will save us a few leftovers."

The women parted ways with Gary and Nash, who climbed into the cab of the truck, giving the women a jaunty wave before driving off.

"Do you think Delta and Gary will ever get serious?" Raylene asked.

"I don't know. They make such a cute couple."

"Kind of like you and Nash," Raylene said slyly.

"Nash and me?" Jo could feel her cheeks redden. "We're mostly friends."

"Mmm. Hmm."

"Don't mmm...hmm me. Delta does that all of the time. It drives me crazy."

"She does it to me too. Delta isn't one to beat around the bush when she's trying to get her point across."

"You got that right."

The women looked both ways before hurrying across the street. Claire was already inside the deli and waved them over.

Jo waved back and began making her way to the table. She was almost there when she caught the eye of another diner - a person she'd hoped to never lay eyes on again.

Chapter 20

Miles Parker was alone, sitting in the corner of Marlee's delicatessen facing out, so he had a bird's-eye view of the entire dining room.

His eyes met Jo's, and she could've sworn the man winked at her. She straightened her back and forced her steps to remain steady as she made her way to Claire's table.

"Hey, gals," Marlee said. "Don't look now, but Parker is in the corner."

"I saw him." Jo pulled out a chair and plopped down. "He winked at me. That man is determined to get under my skin, and I'm not going to let him."

"Any news on the second round of DNA tests?" Claire asked.

"No. My attorney should be calling me anytime now," Jo sighed. "At this point, I've resigned myself to the fact my father is also Miles Parker's father. I'm hoping he and his lawyer will agree there's no reason for Parker to stay in Divine. I pay him off, he takes the money and I never have to worry about him again."

Marlee started to reply and abruptly stopped.

"I know he's going around spouting off about taking this and taking that...mostly my farm. What have you heard?"

"He contacted the listing agent for the old movie theater on the corner."

"Which means he is serious about staying in Divine." Jo's heart sank.

"It appears he's moving in that direction." Marlee glanced over Jo's shoulder. "Maybe he's bored."

"No." Jo could feel Parker's eyes boring into the back of her head, and she knew he was watching her every move. "He seems determined to be a thorn in my side, although I've never done a single thing to him. I couldn't control my father's actions. I never even knew about his existence until he showed up on my doorstep."

"Perhaps negotiations between the attorneys will help," Claire said. "And I think your lawyer should include some sort of agreement that he leaves the area."

"I've already thought about that." Jo reached for a menu. "Now, on to more pleasant topics. Raylene and I are famished."

Marlee waited until the women were ready and jotted down their orders. "I heard the librarian, Jackie White, put Delta in charge of organizing the tables for the baking contest. She's not scheming to gain some sort of advantage, is she?"

Jo shifted in her chair, smiling innocently. "Now, Marlee. You know Delta as well as I do. In fact, you've known her even longer. Do you think she would try to gain some sort of advantage?"

"That's what I thought. What did she do?" Marlee laughed. "Put my designated number in the back corner where no one will see it?"

"No. That would be Amelia Willis," Raylene said.

"Delta Childress," Marlee shook her head.

"And...there might be a slight discrepancy in the size of the entry flags," Jo said.

"Not to mention the color," Raylene reminded her.

"I'm going to march right on over there and switch our numbers around. What's Delta's number?" Marlee asked.

"Number seven. I think you're number eighteen. Delta didn't give you a bad spot. You're wasting your time if you plan to switch them around." Jo's grin widened. "She taped the flags to the table so no one would mess with them."

"Good grief." Marlee wagged her finger. "She'd better watch it, or her shenanigans are going to come back and bite her."

"I agree." One of the other servers waved Marlee over. "I better get back to work."

After Marlee left, the trio discussed the fall festival and the hay maze.

"Gary has done such a great job of putting it together," Claire said. "Speaking of Gary, you breathed new life into him, Jo. Not only has the farm been a lifesaver for women like Raylene, but it's also been a lifesaver for Gary."

"You think so?" Jo twirled the ice in her glass with her straw.

"He's like a new man. I tell you...after Teresa passed on, he was so sad and lonely. We tried to rally round him, making sure we invited him to parties and such, but he seemed to have given up, and then you came along with the farm."

"Jo has the magic touch," Raylene said. "She's like an angel."

"Speaking of angels, have you had any more encounters since you saw the mysterious men by your fence line a couple of weeks ago?" Claire asked.

"No, but it's the oddest thing. Sometimes at night Duke, and I will be in the bedroom, and he'll stare intently, as if he sees someone."

"I think it's an angel encounter," Raylene said. "The other women and I have felt it too."

"Which is why you shouldn't worry about Miles Parker," Claire patted Jo's hand. "God will protect you and the farm."

"I believe you're right, but if you could keep my situation in your prayers, I would be grateful."

"Every day, my friend."

Their food arrived, and while they ate Claire, filled them in on her conversations with Ellen Bice and Woody Stroud. "If either of them is the thief, they'll be hot after the goods tonight."

"So, our sting is at your place for certain." Jo took a big bite of her overstuffed pastrami sandwich, and a dribble of mustard ran down her chin. She closed her eyes and let out a groan. "This is *so* good."

"You can't go wrong with Marlee's food." Claire sipped the hot salty goodness of her chicken noodle soup. "If you've never tasted her chicken noodle soup, you need to give it a try."

Jo, who hadn't eaten since breakfast, gobbled her sandwich and then picked at her French fries to give the other two time to catch up. "I think we should meet you at your house later for the stakeout. It will look suspicious if we caravan out of town."

"Good point." Claire polished off the last sip of soup. "I figured just after nine o'clock is the golden hour. It will be dark by then, giving the culprit a cover if they show up."

"They will," Raylene predicted. "My money is on Ellen Bice since she had the sunflower brooch."

"But Woody Stroud was the one who ran right out to the Clipson estate sale sniffing around for more items," Jo reminded her.

"True," Claire agreed. "We can't rule out Dawn Clipson, either. She knew about the value of the sword after Woody told her. I've been thinking she might have been the thief, somehow convincing herself she wasn't stealing... only taking back what she thought I stole from her client."

"What about the other items?" Raylene asked. "How do you explain the brooch inside Ellen's antique shop?"

"Unless it's a coincidence. Claire told us the brooch isn't unique," Jo reminded her.

"But what are the chances?" Raylene dabbed at the corners of her mouth and tossed the dirty napkin on top of her empty plate. "If one of those three is the thief, I'm certain they'll show up to get their hands on the goods."

"They won't have any trouble finding my place. My home address is public information. I'll be right back." Claire carried the bill to the cashier and returned moments later. She picked up her purse and the small brown box. "I'm going to stop at the laundromat to help close, make sure the antique shop is locked tight and then head home."

Jo eyed the deli's clock. "It will give Raylene and me a chance to stop by the house to check in. Where do you want us to park when we get there?"

"There's a drive along the left-hand side of the house. You can park inside the old red barn out back, just be sure to watch out for my project car."

"Will do."

Raylene and Jo thanked Claire for dinner and returned to the farm where they found Delta in the kitchen standing in front of the sink.

"What are you working on now?" Jo asked.

"My raspberry dessert." Delta wiped her hands on her apron. "This baking contest is gonna be the death of me. How is Marlee?"

"Marlee is fine."

"I mean her demeanor. Is she calm? Is she frazzled?"

"You mean stressed out like you are over the contest?" Jo teased.

"This one's got me in a tizzy," Delta admitted. "I figured if Marlee is cool as a cucumber she thinks she's got this one in the bag."

"I thought you had this one in the bag," Jo laughed.

"Well...I do...I did until Amelia came along." A look of concern crossed Delta's face.

"Marlee seems fine. You'll be fine, too. She was curious about how you arranged the baking contest display to make sure you weren't trying to gain an advantage."

"I would never do that," Delta said.

"Not even giving yourself a slightly larger entry flag and making sure your dish is in a primo spot?" Raylene asked.

Delta shrugged. "I can't help it if one of the flags was slightly larger than the others, and I'm not even sure if my spot is a primo spot. Besides, I gave Marlee a darn good spot, too."

"Yes, you did." Jo's cell phone chimed. "That could be Claire letting us know she's on her way home." She glanced at the screen, and her heart skipped a beat. "It's Chris Nyles. I better take this in my office."

"I'll wait out here," Raylene said.

The phone chirped again. "I'll be right back." Jo darted out of the room and into her office, answering the call as she closed the door behind her. "Hello, Chris."

"Hey, Jo. I have the second set of DNA test results back." Chris hesitated for a fraction of a second before giving Jo the news she already knew. "Miles Parker is related to you."

Surprisingly calm, Jo eased into a chair. "I thought the second set of tests would confirm the fact. Now what?"

"Parker and his attorney received a copy of the results at the same time I did. They haven't wasted any time. Their tentative agreement came via email. Before we start discussing it, I want you to go over it."

"Is it bad?" Jo braced herself.

"It's strong. Parker's attorney is doing what any good attorney worth his salt would do...try to negotiate the best possible settlement. I'm sending it over to you now."

Jo could hear tapping on the other end of the line. "I emailed the cover letter and initial agreement to you. Take your time. I'll wait."

"Thanks." Jo's hand trembled as she opened her emails. Chris's email and an attachment were at the top. She sucked in a breath before double clicking on the attachment.

Her eyes scanned the list, looking for the one thing she feared the most...Parker's attempt to somehow gain control of Jo's beloved farm.

The room began to spin when she reached the last numbered item on the list.

Chapter 21

Jo didn't realize she'd let a small sob escape.

"Jo...are you okay?"

"Yes." She closed her eyes, and a lone tear trickled down her cheek. "Yes. I'm more than okay. Parker and his attorney didn't mention the farm."

"No, and even if Parker wanted it, there's no way he would've succeeded. You purchased the property with your own money years after your parent's estate was settled. He had no legitimate claim to it and would have wasted his time."

Chris continued. "There are some things I would like to negotiate, namely the lump sum to reduce the amount."

"I would definitely feel the pinch." Jo stared at the numbers on the first line and the long row of zeroes behind it. "Obviously, less is better, but I can breathe again, knowing he's not going to try to go after the farm and make my life miserable."

She paused. "There is one thing I do want."

"What's that?"

"I want him gone...gone from my life. Gone from Divine."

Chris interrupted. "He's still in town?"

"Yes, and according to one of the locals, he contacted the listing agent for the old movie theater downtown."

"Why Divine?" Chris asked. "He can take a nice settlement and move anywhere."

"To make me pay," Jo said. "I think he's here to get in my face and in some twisted way to get even with my father."

"I'll put your request at the top of the list." Chris sounded distant. "I have a conference call coming in. Are you sure you're okay?"

"I'm fine. Better than expected."

"Good. Look over the agreement, put together some items you want to see changed, and we'll go over it tomorrow."

"Can it wait until Monday?" Jo asked. "Tomorrow is the kickoff of Divine's fall festival, and I'm going to be busy. Plus, it will give me some extra time to think about it."

"Monday it is." Chris promised to call Jo first thing Monday morning.

After they hung up, Jo stared blankly at the agreement. Miles Parker wasn't going to try to get her farm, but he was still in the area. If Jo agreed to half of the money he and his attorney were asking for, he could buy every single empty building in their tiny town...and be in her face for years.

If nothing else, Jo wanted him to move on, to take his money and live happily ever after...somewhere else.

She was still staring at the screen when there was a light knock on the door.

Delta stuck her head inside. "Everything okay?"

"Yes." Jo nodded her head. "I mean...yes, and no." She told her friend about the test results, the tentative settlement and her conversation with Chris.

"I knew the man was never gonna get his hands on this place." Delta didn't wait for an invitation before plopping into an empty chair. "I wouldn't worry much about him setting up shop here in Divine. And even if he does, we're gonna make him so miserable, he'll pack his bags quicker than you can say skunk breath."

"Make him miserable?"

"Why not? He's determined to make your life miserable...you return the favor. We'll have Marlee slip him a little juju stew and a touch of natural laxative. Add in some of the Kansas Creek Indians secret spice, and he'll be lit up like a firecracker. He'll be afraid to eat in any restaurant within a hundred-mile radius."

Jo smiled at the image of Miles Parker getting in a tight situation and spending his time in the bathroom. "That's not nice."

"And neither is he." Delta abruptly stood. "Looks like now it's just a matter of time before that fancy lawyer of yours hammers out a few details, and Miles Parker is in our rearview mirror."

"I like the sounds of that." Jo slowly stood. "Is Raylene still around?"

"Yep. She's the taste tester for my last official sample of the contest dish. I don't think you'll have time for a taste test before we head out for our stakeout."

"You're going with us?" Jo snatched the car keys off the edge of the desk. "I thought you were too busy."

"Too busy for a little takedown? No way. I want to have a part in catching the culprit. There's no room in this town for riffraff and thieves." Delta stopped when they reached the kitchen doorway. "I'm gonna go grab a pistol. Be right back."

"We don't need..." Jo's voice trailed off. Delta was already gone.

Raylene's chair scraped on the linoleum as she pushed back and patted her stomach. "She's gung-ho to bring her gun."

Delta returned to the kitchen, slowing only long enough to remove her apron and slip on a light jacket. She placed the gun inside her jacket pocket. "I'm ready to roll."

It was a ten-minute drive from the farm to Claire's home. They turned onto her street, and Jo studied their surroundings. The lots were large with ample wide-open spaces in between.

They pulled into the drive of their friend's tidy tri-level, making their way along the left-hand side of the barn and up a small incline before veering onto a rutted path. "Claire told me to park inside the barn out back."

They reached the rear of the property. Jo's headlights illuminated the interior of the barn, as she carefully guided her SUV off to the right, pulling in next to a tarped vehicle. "What's that?"

"It's probably the '59 Chevy Claire is restoring," Delta said.

"A '59 Chevy?" Raylene leaned forward, peering anxiously out the window. "I love classic cars."

"It's a beaut. You'll have to ask Claire to show it to you sometime."

Jo waited for the others to exit the vehicle and locked the doors. They made their way through the backyard to the attached garage's rear entrance, stepping onto the back porch. A motion detector light flashed on.

"We'll have to make sure Claire turns off the motion lights," Delta said. "Otherwise, we might scare off the thief."

The back door flew open, and Claire motioned them inside. "You're right on time. While I was waiting, I called Dawn Clipson to tell her I might consider a higher offer for the sword. If she wasn't willing to negotiate, I was selling it first thing tomorrow morning."

"What did she say?" Jo squeezed past Claire.

"She started cussing me out, and I finally had to hang up on her."

"Good thing I brought something to protect us," Delta patted her pocket. "We noticed your motion lights are on. You may want to turn them off to give the thief time to try to break in."

"Did you notice anything unusual when you got home from work?" Raylene asked.

"No." Claire's hand shook as she reached for the panel of light switches. "I never thought I would be looking forward to someone breaking into my house."

"When you put it like that, it might not have been the best idea," Jo said.

"I want to catch this person. If they got away with it once, they'll do it again." Claire waited for them to set their purses on the kitchen counter before giving them a tour of her home, which was cluttered with antiques and knick-knacks.

The tour ended, and they returned to the kitchen. "I think it's time to get this stakeout underway." Claire turned the interior lights off before positioning herself at the front window.

Delta headed downstairs to the family room with plans to keep an eye on the rear walkout slider and the ground level windows facing the street.

Raylene offered to watch from the third level while Jo stayed close to the garage entrance in case the thief tried to gain entry through the garage.

The house grew quiet as the women watched and waited. The long moments ticked by, and the first hour passed uneventfully. At ten-thirty, Jo decided to check on Claire, who was in the living room. "Anything yet?"

"Nope. Not even street traffic. I've counted maybe four cars." Claire lowered the blind. "Could be the thief decided it was too risky to try to break into my house."

"It's possible," Jo whispered. "I still can't figure out why they sold a potentially valuable sword at a flea market."

"It doesn't make sense."

"Unless...they didn't know the value." Jo pressed her palms together. "But Ellen Bice, Woody Stroud and Dawn Clipson did suspect the sword was potentially valuable. What if we're way off and it was someone else?"

"I was thinking the same thing."

There was a light thumping, and Delta appeared at the top of the stairs. "Anything?"

"Nope." Jo shook her head.

"I almost dozed off standing up."

"Hey!" Raylene's voice echoed in the upper hall. "We got someone on the move."

The women sprang into action, returning to their original positions.

Jo tiptoed to the garage door. She could've sworn she heard the outer door rattle and ran back into the kitchen. The microwave oven gave off enough light for her to search for a potential weapon. She grabbed the first thing she could find...a rolling pin.

There was another rattling sound, and then it grew quiet. Through the murky darkness, she spied Claire darting across the living room.

Thump. Claire lurched forward, flailing wildly as she fought to stay upright. She tumbled to the floor, landing on all fours with a dull *thud*.

Jo ran to her side. "Are you okay?"

"Yeah. Just being clumsy," Claire whispered. "I saw someone sneak around back."

Jo helped her friend to her feet, and they hurried to the dining room slider. Two shadowy figures crept through the backyard toward the downstairs slider. "Downstairs."

Claire and Jo made a move to head downstairs. Before they could get there, a loud *bang* filled the air. Following the *bang* was the sound of angry voices. Delta's voice was one of them.

Jo bolted down the steps, keeping a tight grip on the rolling pin.

Claire was right there with her. She flipped the family room light on and abruptly stopped at the sight of Delta who had a perpetrator pinned to the floor, her gun aimed at the woman's head.

Chapter 22

"Kate?" Claire stared at her laundromat employee in disbelief.

"The other one got away," Delta's chest heaved as she fought to catch her breath. "It was a man."

"I can't believe it. Kate, what are you doing?"

"Get off me." Kate writhed wildly, desperate to break free from Delta's knee which was planted squarely on her midsection.

"Move again, and I'll shoot your ear off."

Kate made a gurgling noise.

"I think she's having trouble breathing," Raylene said.

Delta eased off a little, but the gun never wavered. "Make a move, and I won't hesitate to shoot."

"I'm calling the police." Claire ran up the stairs and returned with her cell phone. "They're on the way. You said there was a second person?"

"Yeah. A man about her age," Delta said. "He ran off when he saw my gun."

"I knew this was a stupid idea." Kate clenched her fists. "Stupid...stupid."

"I agree, it wasn't very smart," Jo said. "So, you're the one who stole the sword from Claire's place."

"I..." Claire rubbed the back of her neck. "Now it makes sense. Kate knew about the sword, too. She saw me carry it to the antique shop the other day and leave it inside. Kate...you left not long after I showed up to finish the shift."

"The perfect crime." Raylene shook her head. "You knew Claire would be working at the laundromat until nine. It gave you plenty of time to break into the antique shop."

Claire interrupted. "You heard me tell Jo I had placed the case under the cabinet. You knew exactly where to find it. You broke in, stole the sword along with some costume jewelry, and sold it to another antique shop."

"I did not." Kate started to say something and then clammed up.

Delta released the safety on the gun, her aim never wavering. "Keep talkin'."

Kate's eyes grew wide, and she nervously licked her lips. "Me and my boyfriend sold it to Bruce, one of the flea market vendors. He's always looking for goods. He took the sword and the jewelry and gave us a couple hundred bucks."

"The flea market guy had no inkling of the possible value of the sword," Jo said. "That's how it ended up with the biker, and then Deputy Franklin found it."

"Bruce," Claire repeated the name. "I think the authorities need to find out exactly what Bruce knows about you and your accomplice, Kate."

Sheriff Franklin and another deputy arrived on scene to take Kate into custody. Nervous and crying, Kate told the sheriff she feared for her life when Delta threatened to shoot her ear off.

"Did you threaten to shoot Ms. Totten?" Sheriff Franklin motioned to Delta.

"Just her ear," Delta said. "She was squirming like a pig wallerin' in slop. I had to do something to keep her still."

"I'm not a pig!" Kate shouted. "You're a pig, not me!"

"And you're going to have a free night's stay on a nice clean cot." The sheriff led Kate out of the house, but not before the young woman told him and the other deputy where to find her boyfriend.

Claire stood in the doorway and watched the sheriff pull out of the drive before closing the door behind them. "I had no idea."

"She had motive and opportunity. But why break in now?" Jo asked.

"Why not? Looking back, she may have been the one messing with the coin boxes, too," Claire said.

Delta shook her head. "It's so hard to find good help these days."

The women hung around until the sheriff called Claire to let her know they had also apprehended Kate's accomplice and boyfriend.

Delta yawned as she waited for her friend to hang up. "I hate to be a party pooper, but we best get going. Tomorrow is going to be a long day."

Claire walked them to the door. "I still can't believe it. Kate of all people."

"You never really know someone," Jo said. "I'm glad it's over for your sake."

Claire thanked them again, promising to keep her cell phone close by in case something else happened.

It was after midnight by the time the trio reached the farm. Delta headed inside while Jo hung back, waiting for Raylene to reach the apartments and Duke took a quick potty break.

After he finished, they followed Delta into the house where Jo made quick work of getting ready for bed.

Despite the late hour and the long day, Jo tossed and turned. She still hadn't taken the time to go over the initial settlement Parker and his attorney had submitted. The most important thing to Jo was her farm...and Parker leaving the area, but that would be something to worry about another day.

She intended to enjoy some time off and the fall festival. And tomorrow evening was Jo's first official date in years...decades.

Would Nash try to kiss her? Her pulse quickened at the thought. Jo hadn't been kissed in years, hadn't missed it, hadn't even thought about it until now.

Duke stretched his paws across the bed and flopped over. "Okay, you bed hog. You have to share." She gave him a gentle nudge, but he refused to budge.

"Fine. I'm too tired to fight." Jo curled up on her side as she mulled over the day's events. Finally, the jumbled thoughts turned off long enough for her to fall asleep.

Duke woke her early the next morning, whining at the bedroom door. "I'm coming." Jo grabbed her bathrobe and stumbled down the stairs to let him out.

After he finished, they wandered into the kitchen. Delta was already dressed and buzzing back and forth from the stove to the counter.

"What time do you have to take your raspberry dessert into town?"

"It has to be there by noon." Delta swiped at her sweaty forehead. "I wanna get there early to make sure no one tries to pull a fast one and move me out of my spot."

"You do what you gotta do. I'll fix breakfast."

"Thanks, Jo."

Jo arranged a layer of bacon in the pan and began frying it while she whipped up a batch of pancake mix. Michelle arrived moments later to help.

Right behind her was Sherry, Kelli, Leah, Raylene and Tara.

Jo did a double take when the women strolled into the kitchen. "All hands on deck," she quipped.

"We figured Delta could use some extra help today," Sherry explained.

"I sure do appreciate it," Delta said breathlessly. "I can't even think straight."

"It's going to be fine." Jo stepped in Delta's path and placed a light hand on her shoulder. "It's a contest. Win or lose, you're always a winner in our hearts."

"Absolutely," Raylene chimed in. "Your raspberry dream bars are the best I've ever tasted."

"Now if only the judges agree." Delta refused to eat, claiming she was too stressed out to swallow a single bite of food. She rushed out the door, forgot her dish and ran back into the kitchen. "I would forget my head if it wasn't attached."

"Do you want me to drive?" Jo offered. "You're a wreck."

"I'm fine."

The back door banged again. Thinking Delta had forgotten something else, Jo sprang from her chair and headed to the kitchen. It wasn't Delta. It was Claire.

"Hey, Claire."

"Hi, Jo. I wanted to stop by before the day got crazy busy and let you know what happened." Claire told Jo that Kate had spilled the beans after the sheriff tracked down the flea market vendor, Bruce.

"Bruce insists he had no idea Kate and her boyfriend were stealing items and selling them."

"But he remembers the sword?" Jo asked.

"Sure does," Claire nodded. "According to Deputy Franklin, Bruce would regularly buy most of the merchandise Kate and her boyfriend brought to him. After buying the items dirt cheap, he would take them to the local antique shops to sell. He decided to hang onto the sword, figuring he could get at least a couple hundred bucks out of it."

"So that's how Ellen Bice ended up with the sunflower brooch," Jo said.

"Yep. Kate and her boyfriend sold it to Bruce, who sold it to Ellen Bice."

"Wow." Jo shook her head. "The thief was right under your nose the entire time."

"Ain't that something." Claire jangled her car keys. "I better get going. I want to open early today. Time is money."

Jo thanked her for the update and returned to the dining room where she wolfed down the rest of her food. After finishing breakfast, the women headed to the bakeshop and mercantile. By the time Jo finished cleaning the kitchen, the day's first wave of customers was already pulling into the parking lot.

The morning flew by, and Jo kept glancing at the clock, wondering how Delta was holding up, how Marlee was holding up and how the baking contest was going.

According to Delta, there were several rounds of competitions...Best in Show. Best taste, most original...and the grand prize - overall most appealing dish.

One of the judges was a local newspaper reporter. The second was a restaurant owner who had a chain of restaurants in Kansas City. The third judge was the newly crowned Smith County Sunflower Queen. The last was a Kansas City television station's food critic.

Finally, Jo couldn't stand it any longer. She hopped in the SUV and drove into town. Downtown Divine was bumper to bumper with cars parked along both sides of the streets.

She drove around for several long moments until finally finding an empty spot blocks away from the community center.

Jo made a beeline for the building, barely squeezing inside where it was standing room only. She bounced onto her tiptoes to try to see what was happening, but all she could see were the backs of peoples' heads.

One of the onlookers glanced at Jo.

"Have they announced a winner?"

"Just now."

"Thanks." Jo eased past the onlookers until she reached the edge of the display tables. Front and center was a woman Jo had never seen before. She was holding a trophy and smiling widely as a local reporter stood nearby, talking to her.

Delta, Marlee and Amelia stood off to the side watching the woman.

Jo made her way over. "She's the winner?"

"Yeah." Delta frowned. "I don't even know who she is."

"She's too young to win," Marlee sniffed.

"I agree," Amelia said. "How on earth did an asparagus and flaxseed bread win the top prize?"

"None of you won?"

"We all got honorable mention and a year's subscription to the Kansas City Star newspaper."

"Well...there's always next year. I need to run back to the farm to pick up the others." Jo had instructed the women to close the businesses at four, giving them ample time to get ready before heading into town to enjoy the festivities.

They were waiting in front of the mercantile when Jo pulled into the drive. She circled around and motioned for them to climb in. "All aboard."

It was a cozy ride, but the women didn't seem to mind as they chattered excitedly. During breakfast, Jo had given each of them fifty bucks to spend, to splurge on the rides, carnival food or anything else that struck their fancy.

Back in town, Jo lucked out and managed to snag an empty parking spot in a field not far from the carnival rides.

While the women headed to the rides, Jo wandered toward the town park. She found Nash and Gary near the entrance to the hay maze.

Jo caught his eye, and Nash made his way over. "Hey, Jo. Is it date night yet?"

"What time is it?" Jo checked her watch.

"Five."

"Then I guess it's close enough to evening."

Nash held up a finger. "Hang on. I'll be right back." He strolled to his truck. Jo watched him reach inside the driver's side window, and then he returned to where she stood waiting. "This is for you." He handed Jo a small box.

"For me?" She slowly opened the box. Inside was a pair of sunflower earrings. "Storm Runner's wife, Namid, made them and she's selling them at their booth."

"They're beautiful." Jo's throat clogged as she tried to remember the last time a man had given her a gift. "I love them."

"I hoped you would." Nash reached for her hand.

Jo carefully placed the small box in her jacket pocket and slipped her hand into his. She struggled to slow her pounding heart but having Nash close made it impossible.

Finally, she started to relax as they strolled out of the park and across the street to the carnival rides.

"Shall we?" Nash motioned to the ticket booth.

"I think I could handle a ride or two," Jo smiled.

"The Ferris wheel it is." Nash purchased a roll of tickets and they headed to the Ferris wheel. Jo climbed in first, and Nash eased in next to her. The narrow seat was barely wide enough for the two of them, and they were so close their legs touched.

Jo's pulse quickened again as their eyes met, and Nash reached for her hand. She forced herself to focus on the view, a breathtaking landscape of brilliant orange, red and purple hues.

"Beautiful, isn't it?" Nash squeezed Jo's hand.

"It is. I love Divine. I never thought I would feel so comfortable and at peace here, or anywhere for that matter." It was difficult for Jo to put into words her exact feelings...she was simply - home.

The ride ended, and Nash convinced her to navigate the house of mirrors, followed by a whirl on the carousel.

Thankfully, the carousel moved slowly. After the ride ended, Nash offered his hand to help her down and motioned to the array of food trucks. "Now that the rides are over let's grab a bite to eat."

The couple walked up and down the aisles, scoping out the different offerings before Jo settled on a thick, gooey slice of pepperoni pizza while Nash claimed he just had to sample a turkey drumstick.

They found an empty spot at a nearby picnic table and munched on their goodies. Several of the women stopped by to chat, breathless and excited by the whirlwind of events.

The couple sampled each other's food, each claiming theirs was the best. After they ate, Jo and Nash returned to the pavilion for a trip through the maze. She let Nash lead the way since she couldn't remember how Raylene and she had gotten out.

Too soon, nightfall set in and the first official day of the festival was winding down.

Jo reluctantly consulted her watch. "I guess I better round up the troops so we can head home."

"Not yet. Gary and I have a surprise. This way." Nash placed a light hand on Jo's elbow and led her to the other side of the pavilion where Delta, Gary and the Second Chance residents had gathered.

"Finally, we've been waitin' on you two," Delta teased. "We figured you were makin' out in the maze."

"Delta Childress." Jo's cheeks turned flaming red.

"You never know," Nash laughed. "I'm never one to kiss and tell."

Jo fanned her face. "Stop. Right now."

"Don't embarrass Miss Jo," Gary turned to Nash. "Are you ready?"

"For what?" Delta asked.

"Our surprise." Gary motioned to the nearby wagon. "We're taking you gals on a bona fide wagon ride."

"You are?" Kelli squealed. "A hayride."

"Climb aboard." Gary placed a wooden crate next to the wagon and helped each of the women climb onboard. Delta and Jo were last.

Gary made his way to the tractor, hitched to the wagon while Nash joined the women and settled in next to his date.

"Ready?" Gary hollered back.

"Let's roll." Nash gave him a thumbs up.

Gary flipped the ignition, and the old John Deere backfired, popping loudly. The wagon lurched forward, causing the wooden boards to groan in protest.

Jo placed a light hand on one of the boards. "Are we gonna make it? This thing sounds like it's on its last leg."

"Nah." Nash waved dismissively. "Gary and I took it out for a test run earlier. The tractor is running like a top."

The wagon jostled and swayed as they began chugging along. They reached the edge of the park, and Gary steered them onto a side street.

Cars passing by on the other side flashed their lights and honked their horns. Each time a car passed the women whooped loudly.

Gary turned another corner onto a quieter street. A sea of stars twinkled brightly overhead, and Jo stared in awe at God's magnificent creation.

There was a chill to the night air, and she snuggled close to Nash, who wrapped his arm around her shoulder and pulled her even closer.

Delta, who wasn't far away, caught the movement. "Time to move away from the lovebirds." She crawled to the other end of the wagon, joining the women, and they began singing.

"Thank you for our date night," Nash whispered in Jo's ear.

He was so close, Jo knew if she turned her head, his lips would be mere inches from hers.

She hesitated for a fraction of a second before slowly turning so their faces were close together. "Thank you for asking me," she whispered back.

Jo started to say something else, but Nash stopped her as he leaned in, his soft lips pressing against hers, and all thoughts were gone.

His lips lingered on hers for a long moment until he reluctantly pulled away. "I think this was a perfect ending to a perfect date."

Jo's heart did a flip as she gazed into his eyes. "I couldn't agree more."

The end.

If you enjoyed reading "Divine Decisions," would you please take a moment to leave a review? It would mean so much to me. Thank you! Hope Callaghan

The series continues... Divine Cozy Mystery book 5, coming soon!

Books in This Series

Divine Cozy Mystery Series

Divine Intervention: Book 1
Divine Secrets: Book 2
Divine Blindside Book 3
Divine Decisions Book 4
Divine Cozy Mystery Book 5 (Coming Soon!)
Divine Cozy Mystery Book 6 (Coming Soon!)

More Books by Hope Callaghan

Made in Savannah Cozy Mystery Series

Key to Savannah: Book 1
Road to Savannah: Book 2
Justice in Savannah: Book 3
Swag in Savannah: Book 4
Trouble in Savannah: Book 5
Missing in Savannah: Book 6
Setup in Savannah: Book 7
Merry Masquerade: Book 8
The Family Affair: Book 9
Pirates in Peril: Book 10
Matrimony & Mayhem: Book 11
Swiped in Savannah: Book 12
Book 13: Coming Soon!
Made in Savannah Box Set I (Books 1-3)
Made in Savannah Box Set II (Books 4-6)

Garden Girls Cozy Mystery Series

Who Murdered Mr. Malone? Book 1
Grandkids Gone Wild: Book 2
Smoky Mountain Mystery: Book 3
Death by Dumplings: Book 4
Eye Spy: Book 5
Magnolia Mansion Mysteries: Book 6

Cruise Ship Cozy Mystery Series

Cruise Control: Book 6
Killer Karaoke: Book 7
Suite Revenge: Book 8
Cruisin' for a Bruisin': Book 9
High Seas Heist: Book 10
Family, Friends and Foes: Book 11
Murder on Main: Book 12
Fatal Flirtation: Book 13
Deadly Delivery: Book 14
Reindeer & Robberies: Book 15
Transatlantic Tragedy: Book 16
Book 17: Coming Soon!
Cruise Ship Cozy Mysteries Box Set I (Books 1-3)
Cruise Ship Cozy Mysteries Box Set II (Books 4-6)
Cruise Ship Cozy Mysteries Box Set III (Books 7-9)
Cozy Mysteries 12 Book Box Set: (Garden Girls & Cruise Ship Series)

Sweet Southern Sleuths Cozy Mysteries

Short Stories Series

Teepees and Trailer Parks: Book 1
Bag of Bones: Book 2
Southern Stalker: Book 3
Two Settle the Score: Book 4
Killer Road Trip: Book 5
Pups in Peril: Book 6
Dying To Get Married-In: Book 7
Deadly Drive-In: Book 8
Secrets of a Stranger: Book 9

Library Lockdown: Book 10
Vandals & Vigilantes: Book 11
Fatal Frolic: Book 12
Sweet Southern Sleuths Box Set I: (Books 1-4)
Sweet Southern Sleuths Box Set: II: (Books 5-8)
Sweet Southern Sleuths Box Set III: (Books 9-12)
Sweet Southern Sleuths 12 Book Box Set (Entire Series)

Samantha Rite Deception Mystery Series

Waves of Deception: Book 1

Winds of Deception: Book 2

Tides of Deception: Book 3

Samantha Rite Series Box Set – (Books 1-3-The Complete Series)

Cozy Mystery Collections

Cozy Mysteries 12 Book Box Set:

Fall Into Murder 6 Book Cozy Mysteries Collection

Audiobooks

(On Sale Now or FREE with Audible Trial)

Key to Savannah: Book 1 (Made in Savannah Series)

Road to Savannah: Book 2 (Made in Savannah Series)

Justice in Savannah: Book 3 (Made in Savannah Series)

Cozy Mysteries Cookbook (FREE Ebook)

Cozy Mysteries Cookbook-Recipes From Hope Callaghan Books

Meet Author Hope Callaghan

Hope loves to connect with her readers! Connect with her today!

Never miss another book deal! Text the word Books to 33222

Visit **hopecallaghan.com/newsletter** for special offers, free books, and soon-to-be-released books!

Facebook: www.facebook.com/authorhopecallaghan/

Amazon: www.amazon.com/Hope-Callaghan/e/B00OJ5X702/

Pinterest: https://www.pinterest.com/cozymysteriesauthor/

Hope Callaghan is an American author who loves to write Christian books, especially Christian Mystery and Cozy Mystery books. She has written more than 50 mystery books (and counting) in five series.

In March 2017, Hope won a Mom's Choice Award for her book, "Key to Savannah," Book 1 in the Made in Savannah Cozy Mystery Series.

Born and raised in a small town in West Michigan, she now lives in Florida with her husband.

She is the proud mother of one daughter and a stepdaughter and stepson. When she's not doing the thing she loves best - writing books - she enjoys cooking, traveling and reading books.

Get New Releases & More

Get New Releases, Giveaways & Discounted Books When You Subscribe To My Free Cozy Mysteries Newsletter!

hopecallaghan.com/newsletter

GiGi's Strawberry Cake Recipe

Ingredients:

Cake

1 box white cake mix

1 - 3 oz. box strawberry Jell-O

1/2 cup water

4 eggs

3/4 cup vegetable oil

1 – 12 oz. bag frozen strawberries (using 3/4 cup for the cake and 1/4 cup for the frosting.

Icing/glaze

1/2 box of powdered sugar (a 16 oz. box)

1/2 stick of butter, softened

1/2 cup of mashed strawberries (double this recipe for extra icing/glaze, and you'll be glad you did)

Directions:

To make cake:

-Preheat oven to 350 degrees.

-Thaw and mash frozen strawberries.

-Combine box of cake mix and Jello.

-Add the water, eggs and vegetable oil and mix for 2 mins on low speed.

-Add 3/4 cup of the mashed, thawed strawberries and mix well until blended.

-Bake at 350 for 50 min in a greased, floured Bundt pan.

To make icing:

-Mix softened butter and powdered sugar until creamy. Add mashed strawberries.

-Cool, then remove cake from Bundt pan and let it continue cooling until warm, not hot.

-Pour icing/ glaze over warm cake.

Made in the USA
Thornton, CO
07/15/23 13:08:58